Publications Presents...

*D*OWN *Low*
IVA

5 Star Publications
3383 Donnell Drive
Forestville, MD 20747

Down Low Diva

ISBN -13: 978-0983247364
ISBN-10: 0983247366
Library of Congress Control Number: 2011937496
First Printing: March 2012

www.5starpublications.net
www.tljbookstore.com
www.facebook.com/authoramandalee
www.authoramandalee.com

Chapter 1

Wearing nothing but my birthday suit and some heels, I drank two shots of Nuvo and smiled with the thought, *'Would Peaches like it?'*, as I reached beside me in my treasure chest to get the two-headed dildo. Loving the feel of it in my hands, my eyes glistened as it flexed as it was shaken. Wanting to get the first taste, I then placed it in my mouth. Sucking tenderly on the big black rubber cock, I got carried away as my body became heated. I walked back to the partially lit doorway where I had left my bitch slave sitting on all fours. As she glanced up at me with those hazel eyes, I showed her the love stick then slapped it in my hand. She got excited. "Who has been a good dog?" I said sexually to her.

She replied happily as she shook her ass, "I have, I have, let me eat, let me eat!"

Taking the prize, I rubbed it on her fine dark ass and then stood in front of her. Watching her breasts sway as she moved aroused me and caused me to think, *I have to give the good bitch a treat, because it has been all week since I felt a hot mouth on me.*

I thought I would lie back against the wall and allow my dog to treat me as if I was an animal running from the hound. Instead, she attacked me by pinning me against the wall. She sat on her butt to watch me spread my legs like an eagle's wings. Opening my pussy lips with a firm hand, my bitch started to taste me. Peaches with her warm mouth, started sucking my clit and tasting my nectar. I could only look down at the top of her head and smile. Like any master giving their animal a small taste of what is to come, I pulled her head back, because having her hair locked around my hand made it easier to start and stop her as needed. Staring into her hungry face, I could see my juices all over her mouth and nose. Looking into her eyes I said, "Greedy dog, you weren't supposed to make a mess. The juice is to be in your mouth, not on your face." She fucking wiped her face and licked her hands to get all of me in her.

When I tried to walk off, she grabbed my thighs with her hands, pleading, "Give me another chance? Give me another chance? Please, please let me serve you?"

Satisfied with her answer, I responded, "That's more like it, but you were a bad dog." Moving away from the wall, I walked behind her and spanked that big ass of hers a few times. She watched me go into the heavily-lit living area. Being the good dog I know

Peaches can be, she followed me on all fours. Taking advantage, I squatted on the living room table and told my dog to come eat out of the doggy bowl. From the back, she spread my ass, laid her head on the table between my open legs, and licked and sucked my pussy. Taking her on a new ride, I fucked her mouth and could have sworn I bruised her because of the way she was putting it on me. I really wouldn't have given a fuck. I couldn't move because the rushing cum came fast and flowed all over her.

Before I could get up, she moved her head and used her tongue to fuck my ass and lick down to my already dripping wet pussy. This is a level that bitches usually don't put me on, but I got caught up because Peaches used her tongue increasingly in my ass, and when I had had enough, I flipped around and she started sucking my cum off the table. If you knew Peaches like I do, you would know she is very skilled and highly trained in eating pussy and licking ass; she was the best. "Too bad that hot mouth of yours goes to waste. Teach your husband how to do it." I said to her. She stopped and tried to tell me about Pete, her husband, but I got up, sat on the couch, and checked her. "Silence! Did I give your ass permission to stop tasting me or to talk? If you stop again, you may go home. Now shut up and eat!" I opened my legs wide as if to measure the couch, and like a trained house pet, she didn't miss a beat. It felt so good to feel her tongue dipping in and out of my pussy, especially the way she made it curve. *I need to take this bad*

bitch back home to Forest with me. Then again, Pierre would be so pissed off. I'm already bringing one female home; he'll shit bricks if I brought home two. Then again, the way she's taking care of business, Pierre might be fucked, I thought. "All right, you want to be a real good dog?" I told my favorite girl.

"Anything for you," she said in a naughty tone.

I instructed her to lay back, and she did. Not knowing what to expect, I said, "Play in that pussy for me."

In a ripping-like motion, she tore off the panties, and with her legs wide open, her pretty black fingers began to play in that pussy. In and out she would take her fingers, and on them was the honey. She knew I was watching, and to tease me, she licked her fingers and put them back into her pussy.

"How does it taste?" I asked.

She replied, "Not as good as you."

I smiled, knowing she was not lying. Noticing how well she followed directions, I thought with devilish intentions, *There's nothing like having a bitch do what you want her to do.* Focusing back on Peaches, I continued to watch her juices flow from her pussy to her butt, and this made me ready to give her the present. "Stop," I told her, and she did. Grinning, I pulled out the prize and she licked her lips. I got up, straddled her, and placed one end in her mouth. With my left hand I held the other end in mine. We both were sucking, but to increase the motion, with my right hand I

played in her pussy. I needed to show her who was the bad bitch, and that she wasn't going to outdo me. Seeing that she was enjoying it too much, I got up and told her to lay still. Placing my butt on the carpet, I scooted to her, and with her legs gapped, I placed them over mine.

Glancing back into her face, I noticed she was moaning as she squeezed her breasts. As I used the toy to play around her pussy, she would move her head back and forth, while her body swayed to the teasing touch. She was anticipating my next move. Realizing that she was becoming delirious, I said, "Here comes the good part." I took the huge dildo and entered her slowly. She began to rock her body to the masculine feel between her legs, so I pulled it out and she made whimpering sounds.

"Shh baby," I told her, "you're going to get some more. I just had to punish you first for talking out of turn."

Purposely, I hesitated just to make her wait, and then a little roughly, I entered her on one side and placed the other side inside my pussy and slid Peaches to me. The dildo was completely out of sight, and the moment our pussies touched, we began to grind and roll our bodies uncontrollably on each other. By the way she moved, I could see that she was into it because her legs became tight and she started to shake. I began to think, *Yeah, I'm about to find out just how bad this bitch really is.* Taking my hands, I cuffed them under her legs. By doing this, I pulled her even closer and banged her body harder against my pussy. All she could do was moan and grunt loudly. Smiling, I thought, *If we had neighbors to see this, they too would get off on this scene and we wouldn't even care.*

Putting my mind back on Peaches, she began to bite her bottom lip harder and with her eyes closed, heavy passion was taking over. To stay in control of us in the middle of our fucking, I slid back and told her to lie still. Looking down, I could see she had more of the dildo in her than I did. *That greedy bitch, she's going to buck out of control for that*, I thought as I touched my wet and sticky end. In an enticing way, I ever so slowly slid the dildo out of her pussy, spanked her naughty pussy with it, and a small orgasm escaped her pussy lips. Seeing this sight made me realize that I had to take this bitch on a major thrill, because being a bad bitch myself like I know I can be, I decided to take this bad bitch to another level, and how high, was completely up to her.

Getting up off the floor, she asked reluctantly, "You done?"

Admiring the sight displayed before me, in reply I told her, "Get on all fours on top of the table." Not sure where I was going with this move, Peaches followed my directions. *Oh how I like how her pretty black ass spread*, I thought, then out loud I told her to spread them. Amazingly, she was low and almost parallel to the table. I still had to say, "Look at this bad ass fucking bitch showing the fuck out." I sucked on one end of the dildo again just to taste

her juices, and slower than ever I plugged the head of the dildo in her ass, while the other one was in her pussy. At first she grunted and shook, but she took that dick as I worked both ends in her with my right hand like a virgin working his meat for the first time. Then I used my left hand to hold myself up while I licked around her ass and pussy. *Damn, her pussy was sweet and wet*, I thought as a sexual atomic bomb built up in me. The more she sounded pleased, the more I worked her and licked her, but I was getting too heated again; I needed to mellow myself out just for a minute.

I pulled the dildo out and she asked, "What you doing?"

I screamed at her, "Shut the fuck up and flip over on this table!"

My good dog did it like I knew she would, and at that moment my cup of tea was in sight from earlier. Facing my inside palm to me, I poured the ice onto my hand, put the ice in my mouth and crushed it. Going into a circular motion I felt the ice linger on my tongue tip, so I bent down and played ice hockey with Peaches' pussy. To make her explode was my goal. She jumped as I used the ice to my advantage to suck on her hot clit. Finally, I broke this bad bitch down.

The surprise my ears heard was, "Oh My God, shit, what the hell you trying to do to me?" Without any warning, she yelled with pleasure as she came.

★ ★ ★ ★ ★ 7

Tasting her filled me and I had to taste it all. Showing her how the bad bitch in Mississippi takes care of business, I sucked her up. When I got finished with her, she lay there in a trance, and I spoke more harshly than ever. "Bad bitch! Shut up, did I tell you to talk? Now get off the table and lay on your stomach." Weakness and nervousness overtook Peaches, because when she got up she fell. Pleased with myself, I got beside her and rubbed her back to soothe her, as her nerves jumped at my touch.

Dangling of keys and a knock at the door startled us both, and into our sight came Jimmy. His eyes slowly raked over our naked bodies as he closed the door. Grinning and grabbing his dick, he responded with laughter. "You bitches didn't call me over to fuck, you sneaky bad bitches."

"I didn't think you wanted to play with a bunch of bad dogs because we bite," I said as I got off the floor. Looking at Peaches, I said, "Go get dressed and go to your husband and kids. Next time I come to town, we're all going to play, is that understood?"

Walking closer to me, she kissed me and replied, "To the bad bitch, anything you say." She got dressed then walked out the door.

"Jimmy, did I order take-out today?"

Smiling, he replied, "No, I decided to bring it to you for free."

I looked at his crotch and remembered that he was small, and after the black dildo, I needed more than what he had to offer. I got the food and escorted him out the door because I had another engagement coming up and I didn't have time to fuck off with him.

I went in the bathroom to clean myself up. Soaking in the tub, I could still feel Peaches and how she did the damn thing to me. Truly, she had put something on my damn mind, and honestly, she had blown it away. I got dressed, put on some smell-good and waited for him, because whenever I am in town, he comes running.

Chapter 2

School girls and regular house wives go to bed early, while bitches like me stay up, ready to fuck. We can't go to bed doing only the missionary position or regular doggy style, freaks like me need more, and going to bed early is not it.

I opened up my luggage and thought about what to wear for Peter. I brought along a few new items in my wardrobe, but I needed something that said, "Spank me, I've been a bad kitty." Over to my right, the nurse uniform was nice but there also was the two piece cat outfit. I almost forgot about that one, but when I saw the pleasure-getter, it screamed "I bite." Getting in front of the mirror, I rubbed my body down with strawberry motion lotion. Carefully, I parted my hair down the middle and tied a ball on each side. Glancing back to the mirror, I had to make sure they were even, and they were. Placing my cat ears on my head, with ease I

drew cat whiskers on my face with eye liner and smothered my lips with red lipstick. Taking a napkin, I kissed it to remove the excess.

After putting on my cat face, the top was a natural because the only part covered was the nipples. Noticing my bald pussy, I put on the candy and continued to admire my own firm and plump breasts. They looked damn good, and I just had to rub them and give them a slight squeeze. Touching myself caused pleasure to come out of my mouth. I thought seductively, *I need to save this for Peter*, but the thought of touching my pussy made me question, *Why not fuck yourself? You look good enough to lick clean.* Anyway, Peter was taking too long, and my decision was to become my own meal. I lay across the bed, closed my eyes, and started caressing my breasts. Halfway through the breast touching, I heard a knock at the door. Glancing at the clock on the wall, I knew it had to be Peter, and if it wasn't, whoever it was, they were fucking me.

I looked over at the table and had to make sure I had hand cuffs, silk bandanas, whipped cream, rope, and yes, edible lotion, the key ingredients to rock a world. Thinking about Peter's cock, I looked at the three thick dildos on the table and thought, *Just in case he goes limp tonight, he can choose the one he wants to use on me.* Getting up off the bed and liking the setting on the table, I had to make sure my whip was ready; therefore, I smacked it in the air. My eyes increased when I heard the cracking sound, for it made me shiver and reminded me why I like fucking Peter. He has eight stout inches and a mushroom cap to make me run for the hills. His pure beef stick would bang me out of control, and often times he has my sexy ass hollering.

After all this licking and eating ass, I needed a down-home fucking, and if Peter brings it like he usually does, I will not be disappointed. Not to keep my good dick waiting, I went to the door. It was Peter, so I turned the lights off and opened the door.

When he came in, I said, "Don't turn the lights on, you're in my world now." I locked the door behind him and I stated, "You stopped me from fucking myself; you're going have to make that up."

I felt his eyes on me as he replied, "That's not a problem too big for me to take care of."

Leading my jungle ape to the bedroom, I felt his hard dick and knew that tonight I would be the only tree he swung on. Very close to his ass, I smacked the whip and he jumped, so I commanded him to strip and lay his naked ass on the bed. With my hands, I handcuffed him first and then tied his feet apart to each bed post.

Glancing around for anything else I needed, I put the silk bandana in his mouth, just in case he got a little too loud. Peter saw the whip in my hand and started to buck, because the last time I actually hit him, but tonight I will torture him to think I will.

★ ★ ★ ★ ★ 12

"Calm down, my ape, I'll let you come out to play," I said teasingly.

Picking up the lotion, I oiled him down, then got between his legs, just above the belly button and licked my way up. Chills were seen all over the tied-up animal, but I had to continue. At the nipple area, I teased them, and they too became rock-hard, but that was the beginning and not the attraction yet. Getting back off him, I got the whipped cream and made a trail from both feet to the center point. With ease my tongue did the walking and his toes wiggled in my mouth. With each toe I sucked, the more intensely he pulled against the bed.

At one point, he began to levitate his lower body as if he was sticking me; therefore, I got up and said, "Be still my ape, I have you in captivity. People have been complaining about an animal on the loose, and now that I have you, I must punish you for frightening the people." Picking up the whip, I turned it sideways then started smacking it all across him, and with sound of the whip, his eyes became big with fear and he would jump. "Let me give you something to calm you back down." Releasing the whip, I got between his legs and continued the trail to the center point. Near the point of my destination, I licked stringy fur and cream. He began to calm down, but it wasn't until I arrived at the destination that he became obedient as I took him fast for a few moments, then

I rocked my head slow. I wasn't ready for him to blow, so I got up and untied him.

"If you think what you did to me was something, just wait," he said with a smile.

He stood in front of me, now naked. This cat got on her knees and touched his stern dick, saying, "You feel as if you haven't been emptied in a few days?"

As he grew in my hands, he replied, "I knew you were coming and were in need of a wildcat, not a house cat."

He pushed me on the bed and began to eat away at my edible thongs. His mouth made every part of me water and thrive for his goodness. Feeling me throw it to him, his head bounced with every rock of my pussy; he was catching everything I threw to him. Peter lifted his head up and crawled on top of me. With each leg residing in the east and west, he pounded me nonstop, and calling his name, I did nonstop. For some reason tonight, I took that dick like a solider and proving myself was just the beginning.

"I'm not ready to release, I have a lot for you tonight," I heard him say.

He reached on the table and picked up the small cock. Seeing my eyes grow with desire, he placed the other nicer-sized cock to my mouth and I began to suck it. The further he went from my mouth with the cock, the more I reached for it with my head. Following the cock to the floor, he guided me to the tub

blindfolded and he instructed me to reach up with my hands. I did. Without being told what to do, I then stood on the edge of the tub with my legs trying to do a split, but the walls held me up.

My body was open to whatever hole Peter wanted to use. Although I was nervous, I knew no matter what hole he chose, it would be good. He got the whip and smacked it by me. I jumped. He waited a few more minutes and smacked it again, and this time I screamed with excitement. I heard him drop the whip on the floor, and he took his hands and started to feel each of my legs. As he made his way to my ass, I began to moan with readiness, but he kept me in suspense. Taking his hands, he lightly touched my breasts with eagerness. He sat on the edge of the tub under me and began to slowly eat my pussy. *Peter knows how to take his time and please a bitch when he wants to, and tonight he has given me the best of him*, I thought, but thinking about what he was doing was late, because with his mouth, he went to the bottom and eased his way to the mouth of the pussy.

Once on the top, he tenderly sucked the clit, and small traces of juice ran down my legs. He saw the leakage and stood back behind me, and continued to lick the trails of juices from my ankles to my pussy.

"Oh, Peter!" I cried out.

This tender loving would make a weak bitch fall in love, and he needs to recognize that I am not it, but oh how close I can be.

He then put his thumbs under my ass cheeks and opened them up. Peter used his fingers to lock in place the grip he had on my ass. As he massaged my ass sides, he put his head in my ass, and using his wide tongue, he licked my booty clean. Amazing, so amazing, is the only word to describe how too damn good this felt.

When he finished his dinner on me, he said, "Christina, tonight you will remember that you don't need a fake dick."

As I stood there stunned by that remark, he placed a dick to my mouth and said, "Sniff it." He placed the nice-sized cock to my mouth and I began to suck it. Taking it away, he said, "Kitty Kat, you left hair all over my furniture and bed. You shed your fur, bad kitty."

He took the long bumpy dildo and slowly inserted it into my pussy. I thought I would die with pain, but the pleasure overtook me. Using the dildo to play hide and seek, he hid the long, bumpy, thick cock inside my pussy. He went in and out of me like a professional violinist, using my pussy as the strings. Each time he would slowly back the bumpy dildo out of me, I would scream out in pleasure. When he would hide it again, I would tighten my ass cheeks, but he would slap them and say, "Let go," and somehow I would.

I couldn't touch him or the dildo with my hands, and it was torture. This time Peter took the pleasure out of me and put it in

my mouth and said, "Now you are a good kitty, tasting yourself because that is what good cats do."

I tasted good, and I hungered for more of the taste, but more for his taste. After grueling moments of taking the cock in the pussy, he put it in my ass. Like a budding flower, my ass opened up to bloom. Peter would go slowly, then fast, causing me to scream, moan and rock with the pleasure he was giving me. When he let me go, he didn't waste time to get this Grade-A pussy.

Peter toted me out the bathroom and took me straight to the bed. He looked into my face and said, "I see that pussy purring already."

I gripped my legs around his waist as he went deeper and deeper inside of me. It felt so damn good. Peter rammed his dick in my pussy so hard. I jumped, but he held me by the shoulders and rode me like a horse. I spread my legs farther out and bounced on that dick. I wished Peaches could see a real bitch get fucked. As if he was a thief, he quickly turned me over and busted his nut on my ass cheeks. To return the favor, I turned around and sucked the rest of the cum out of his dick. He loved that shit; even though his dick was sensitive, I sucked slowly.

At two a.m., I drank all Peter had inside him, and then he went limp and crawled into the bed. It was four a.m., and while Peter slept, I bathed and smiled, because not only do I have one qualified lover, I have two, and they happen to be husband and wife. *A lucky bitch I am...* But interrupting my thoughts was Peter. He said he was leaving before Peaches got up, and I told him he needs to tell her, because I want them both in bed.

He said, "Peaches is more into women like I am." Then he looked at me, and I guess after he thought of the both of us giving him a joy ride to remember, he agreed in a hurry.

Before leaving, Peter put his hand in the water and placed his big finger in my pussy. He was giving me a finger quickie, and when he pulled it out, he sucked his finger, and there is nothing sexier than a grown-ass man tasting my pussy and my bath water. Then he said, "You taste good this morning."

I knew all too well that he has my pussy on his mind and not his wife's. The place was quiet, and I thought about my husband and wife team. *As good as Peter is, I don't know why Peaches won't let him fuck her like that, but I have a surprise for her ass. No slow rolling, no grinding shit, just straight up banging the pussy, and that thought alone has me ready for the return trip.*

My flight was due to leave at two p.m., and at ten a.m. I was alone and surprisingly horny as hell. "I just had a woman and a man. Why the hell is my lower half still aching for more?" I thought when I heard a knock at the door. Barely covering up, I peeped out and it was Peter and Peaches. My face lit up like a kid on Christmas morning. Quickly, I opened the door and they came in. Peaches kissed me when Peter turned his back and said, "I

missed you baby." Touching her firm dark ass, I had missed her too damn much. I was thinking, *oh, it's on now.*

As Peaches went into the kitchen, I thought they both wanted to see me off, and I couldn't blame them. *Good pussy and great dick...what a winning combination...* but with the suspicious look in Peter's eyes, I had to ask. "So you both came over here to fuck me. Is that what you're saying to me?" As he led me into the familiar bedroom, I lay in the bed naked and he said, "No, I'm fucking you while she is cooking us breakfast."

"I see." Then I continued sadly, "Peter, I want her to join us."

A greedy look was all on his face and he said, "Maybe when you come back, but right now I want you again. All to myself."

Then he climbed on the bed and pulled the covers back. My pussy was exposed; ready for him to take me. Before he could touch me, my pussy began dripping like a water faucet. Taking his forefinger, he wiped away my cum and he licked his lips. "Sweet, sweet, sweet, look at that pretty ass cum running down your ass." Not able to contain himself, Peter rushed down on that pussy and began licking me up like he was eating a biscuit with syrup. He licked for a few minutes and then mounted on top of me.

When he stuck that big dick inside of my wet pussy, I just moaned out loud. He began to take small strokes, then faster and faster. Before long, he was banging that pussy like on a porn flick. I gripped my legs around his waist as he went deeper and deeper

 19

inside of me. It felt so damn good. I opened my eyes to see Peaches standing at the door, watching us fuck. Opening my legs up wider so he could go deep, I wanted her to see how I wanted her to take that dick when I came back. She was going to get off that dick. We started stroking and stroking at each other. Peter rose up and flipped me over. I turned around facing the doorway, so he could see his wife watching us. Peter looked up at Peaches and rammed his dick in my pussy so hard. I jumped, but he held me by the shoulders and rode me like a horse. I spread my legs farther out and bounced on that dick. I couldn't even imagine…*How she have all those kids and don't have much experience at fucking? Peter was the first man she ever fucked and she stuck with him.* I was surprised he hadn't torn the bottom out that pussy. After we fucked for about thirty more minutes, Peaches returned to the kitchen to prepare breakfast. After that morning workout, we showered and went to eat breakfast. "Peaches, did you enjoy the show?" I asked her.

"Yes baby, I did."

"That's how I want you to fuck Pete when I get back. Or you can do it while I'm gone? He likes the rough sex. Fuck him," I told her.

"Okay baby," she replied while staring at Pete. He didn't even look up at her.

"Pete, what's wrong with you," I asked.

"Nothing baby, shit, I'm just eating. I'm hungry than a mutherfucker."

"Well, can I fuck you both when I get back?" I asked him. "Hell yeah, you know I want to fuck you both. Didn't know you was fucking my wife without me?" he spoke, trying to play it off.

"Nigga, stop fucking playing. I have been fucking you both for a year now."

"Damn Christina, you been fucking her longer than you been fucking me?" he asked,

looking surprised.

"Yes, what's wrong with that nigga? Don't play no fucking games. You are going

to get a chance to fuck us both when I return. It doesn't matter how long I've been fucking who," I stated.

Pete just shook his head and kept eating. Peaches sat down and we all ate breakfast together. After we finished, Pete gave me a kiss on the cheek and they rushed off.

After breakfast with my lovers, I felt tired as hell. Fucking with his wife, and then fucking off with him… "A bitch like me need Vitamin C, not D and P." I laughed as I said that. Gathering my things, I looked around, because leaving Denver was always hard, but I always had the memories to keep me until I got back. My eyes looked at the table and the floor, and instantly replayed the events with Peaches and Peter. I fixed my make-up, packed my bags, and when the cab came to take me to the airport, I left.

Chapter 3

I boarded the plane looking for Paris and I didn't even see her. Bitch didn't even call me to say if she was still going to Mississippi or what. Angrily, I thought, *If this bitch friend of mine is going to play games, I could have taken my real bitch Peaches, but hell no, she got kids.* I looked at my cell phone, and it was dead like a mutherfucker. "What the hell was I thinking to not charge my phone?" Not thinking about my phone, I began to think more about the pussy that was to go with me. Walking up and down the plane, I still didn't see her, but I was trying to be optimistic. I just figured she caught another flight, because she wouldn't dare miss a chance to come down and fuck off with my people.

The plane began to take off and people were sitting and eating their food, and I could only think about Paris, and where the fuck she could be. As I stared out the window, the young lady that sat

next to me kept licking her lips. She had blond hair, blue eyes, sexy as hell and smelled good. Her breast looked ripe and I could see myself tasting those pink nipples. I didn't want to seem obvious, but I guess she can feel who is in and who isn't. Feeling the same, I used my head and pointed towards the bathroom. She went in first and stripped, and then I walked in after her.

Once inside the confined area, she sat on the sink with her ass inside the sink and said "You look like you need some cheering up, so wash your face." I took my hand and inserted it inside her pretty pussy. She moaned a little. Each time I took my fingers out of her, I would add another one. Each finger added would cause her to move her ass a little. I could see she was already raining wet with fever, so I played a little longer with her. Leaning forward, I took those pretty tits in my mouth one at a time.

Her moaning escalated and I said, "You have to be quiet, we don't want any disturbance from the attendants," and she muffled the sounds. Going down to her navel, I played with her belly ring and thought, *How fascinating, I may get one*, but I couldn't stop there, my mouth wouldn't let me. I lightly rubbed her pussy and she purred. I took her pussy lips between my fingers and pulled on them, and she gasped. With her smell good and the way I was feeling, I slowly placed my mouth on her clit and sucked it. She almost kicked me, but from her position she couldn't even move, so she had to lay back and take this tongue. In and out, out and in,

 24

my tongue played the dick, and each time I went inside her, she squeezed my face, allowing me to have her scent in my nose, but right now it didn't even fucking matter. The tighter she squeezed, the tighter I sucked. It was so good she tried to run, but she couldn't move. I was in front of her and she was pinned down. Her watery sugar was all over my face, but I continued to please her.

She begged me to stop, but I couldn't. I was thinking of Paris and how she was missing out on the feeling that I was giving another woman. The lady kicked her legs, but I still wouldn't stop; if she was a well, I was going to drink her dry. Her legs became limp, and that didn't bother me. I still insisted on taking my tongue in and out of her pussy, and going as far down her ass as I could. She hit the walls and begged with what breath she had for me to stop.

I looked up at her and said, "Bitch, you gave me the ticket so enjoy the ride." With that, I went back in to her even slower, because I took her too fast and her cum was running wet. I was looking for the sticky wet, so I would know that she had enough. I took the tongue and went all around her clit, and she bucked harder into the sink, so I placed her legs on my shoulders to keep the noise down. It worked, because with me locked in, I had clear access to all her sweet-tasting goods. I wasn't quite finished drinking her up, but when I leaned back some, she just sat in the sink with her pussy and breasts fully exposed to my view.

I took all five of my fingers and eased them inside her and she moaned but said, "I've had enough, please let me up, it's too good, way too good." Looking into the strange woman's face, I saw Peaches and I had to have some more.

Taking each pussy lip into my mouth, I sucked them pink, and the second lip seemed more swollen than the first, but I was carried away by the smell of her and the way she tasted. I said, "Let me get a little more, and I will leave you alone."

What else could she say? I had her in a position where she couldn't even move to save her own damn life. Just as I promised, a little bit longer and I let the good-smelling, nice-tasting bitch go. I had done my good deed for the day. I took the toilet paper and wiped my face and hands off. Turning around, I opened the door and left. She was still propped up in the sink the way I left her, and all I could do was smile.

Going back to my seat, I looked out the window at the sky and was waiting for the woman to come back. Halfway through the flight, she walked slowly and sat down. I leaned towards her and said, "I was beginning to wonder when you were coming back?"

She gave me a faint smile and replied, "You're one bad bitch. Can I have your number, or will you take mine?"

I grinned and replied, "Sure, I'll take yours, just don't forget about me if I call."

She looked at me and said, "After the way you handled that, there is no way I would forget." We enjoyed the rest of our flight in peace. The time had come for us to stand up. She turned to me and said, "The next time, I'm going to show you how bitches like me get down."

Nodding my head, I was at a loss for words, because if you say something like that to me, you better be able to back it all the way up. Finally, an hour later, I arrived in Mississippi. The taxi cab picked me up. Pierre wanted to be there, but he had to take care of business. My parents were coming back in from out of town themselves. It didn't bother me that I had to catch a fucking cab. Arriving at the hotel; I decided to unpack my shit and take a shower. I wanted to play with myself, but my pussy was already open. I douched with some Summer's Eve vinegar type, hoping it would tighten my shit back up. Damn, I didn't feel like arguing with that nigga tonight. Then again, he probably didn't give a fuck. I lay patiently in the cherry Queen Anne bed wearing the pink lace Victoria's Secret lingerie, while waiting on Pierre. I was very excited, because I hadn't seen him in months and he was about to lay some dick to me. Pierre is a smooth black chocolate brotha with gold on each side of his mouth, brown eyes, braided hair to the back, and abs that seem to wave at you. Even though he had all of this going on, he dressed like he was important. He would tell me that bitches wanted him; I didn't think so, but all my hating ass

enemies were after him. Oftentimes when he and I were out, bitches would come out from the woodworks just to check out my man.

The Scott County Police Department thought Pierre was a dope boy. He had mad money, but he got it from his parents. They left him with a 10 million dollar life insurance policy each. A drunk driver killed them in 2005 late one Christmas Eve while they drove home with gifts. That was a year ago, and Pierre was alone. Luckily, I was by his side before he got all this money. I didn't want people to think I was in it for the money. I really loved Pierre. Stepping out the shower, I had to relax. I had done a lot of shit since I last saw my baby, and now tonight was his time. No Peaches, no Peter, and no good-smelling bitch on the plane were going to make me lose focus of what I had to do tonight.

The weather seemed dreary and I had to rest, but waiting on my man was important. Suddenly the thunder roared very loudly outside. I jumped out of the bed to look out the window. Pierre was driving from Madison County, and I started to worry about him. As I looked out the window, the rain beat against the windowpane as if it was trying to get in. Lightning flashed and I jumped back. I turned to look towards the door, and in walked Pierre. He was looking so handsome.

"My baby," he said as he put down his bags.

I didn't say a word, I just ran to him and put my arms around his neck. Pierre closed the door before I jumped all over him. He stood straight up to lift me in the air. He placed his hands between my legs, opening them wide until he cuddled my ass. We began to share a passionate kiss, his tongue in my mouth as I placed mine in his. My body got weak while he carried me over to the bed. Before he placed me on the bed, we stared into each other's eyes.

"I miss you so much, baby," he spoke softly.

"Baby, I miss you too. Take me and make love to me, like it's our first time."

"I promise I will, and more."

He laid me down on the bed and placed his hard chocolate body on top of me. I felt his hard dick through his pants. He lifted his body off mine and took off his shirt, while staring me in the eyes.

I began to pull my shorts off and he spoke, "No, let me do it."

I lay there being impatient. I wanted him to push dick deep within me. Pierre took off my shorts and rubbed my shaved pussy. As I lay there on the bed, I began to get very wet. He bent down on the bed and began to eat my pussy. He would always smell me and then stick his tongue deep. "Uuugggghhh."

I let out a low sigh as he stuck his tongue deeper and deeper, making me cum everywhere. He placed a finger in my pussy and

his tongue caressed my clit. He sucked and licked me for quite awhile.

"Baby, let me do you," I spoke.

He stood up and took off the rest of his clothes. As he did that, I pulled off my top and bra. My perky breasts were out and my nipples were standing straight up ready to march. Wow, his dick stood out so long and hard. Pierre was about nine inches, and I loved it. He stood staring at me, stroking his dick, ready to fuck me.

"Come suck this dick baby."

"Here I come, big daddy."

I slid to the edge of the bed and he put his dick all in my face. I slightly bent down on my knees while my elbows rested on the bed and began to lick the head of his shaft. Pierre let out a low moan. I took that dick in my hand and began sucking him slowly. I wanted to hear him moan and groan for me. He grabbed the back of my head and pushed deeper into my mouth. There were a couple of times that he made me gag, but I continued to suck my baby like no tomorrow. He missed me sucking him off every day.

I wanted to continue sucking Pierre, but he placed me back on the bed and put his dick deep within my pussy. I moaned so loudly because it had been such a long time since we fucked. He pushed little by little until he worked it all the way inside me. I wrapped

my legs around his hips as he began to stroke me. He pulled out and came all over my stomach.

"Damn baby, that was very quick," I joked.

"Christina, it's been a very long time since I fucked you. And plus, I see my dick is white; so somebody got their nut too."

I punched him in the arm softly. Pierre lay back on the bed while I got up to clean off. "Where are you going?"

"To the bathroom."

"Hurry up, because I want to lay more pipe to that pussy all night. You caught me off guard. You cheated. You rolled that pussy and made me shoot early."

"Boy please, you know you a minute man."

"Yeah right, bring that pussy back and we'll see about that."

I wiped off my stomach and hurried back to get more loving. He's going to fuck the hell out of me for making that joke. It's all good, because I was due for a good fucking. "Here I come, big daddy."

"Bring daddy that pussy," Pierre spoke softly as he stroked himself, waiting. He jumped off the bed and grabbed me around the waist. "I want to hit that pussy from the back."

I placed my knees on the bed with my ass in the air. Pierre put his hand on my ass and pushed me down on the bed. I lay flat on my stomach as he entered me. He had to take it slow at first, and then he gave me the business. He fucked me like he just got out of

prison. He stroked that pussy until I felt weak in the knees. He flipped me over and put my legs on his shoulders and wore this pussy out. I tried to fuck back, but he was putting so much pressure on me that I couldn't move. You could hear that dick slapping against my pussy. Pierre took my legs down. He began to stroke me slowly while looking into my eyes. I lifted my hips to every stroke. I took that entire dick deep. He knew that was how my pussy got satisfied. He made me cum about six times before he got off again.

I believe we screwed all night long. We finally fell asleep around four in the morning. I cuddled up in Pierre's arms like a baby. He made me feel so good. I had a very good man. That's why all of them whores were after him, because they knew he was a good man. Half those bitches wanted him for his money. Money didn't make the world go 'round. He knew that he had a good woman too. Fuck that, I had a man and money on my side. Any bitch that got in my way, I took care of it. I was ready to fight for my man. He said that I didn't have to worry about them bitches, but I had to let them know that Christina De'Angelo wasn't any pushover. I was standing my ground.

We stayed at the Hilton Hotel the whole weekend. He wanted it to be special for me when I came home instead of the same old place. He lived in a big mansion in the Annandale Community out in Madison. I lived in Forest, in the Chapel Hill Community. He

wanted me to move in with him, but that shit wasn't going to happen. My parents worked too hard to buy this house for me.

"Christina, have you thought about what I asked you?"

"No, not really."

"Why not? I really want us to move in together."

"Boy, you know I'm not about to move in with you. We have been going through this for about a year now. Why you keep asking me?"

"I really need you in my life; I want to make you my wife."

"Don't do this to me."

"Do what?"

"Pierre baby, can we talk about this later?" I spoke as I walked up to him and put my arms around his neck, giving him a passionate kiss.

That usually makes the conversation go away. His dick would get hard and we would fuck like dogs. But this time it didn't work.

"It's not going to work this time, baby. I really love you, and I had time to think about this while you were away at college. I'm so fucking glad you are finished."

"You are beginning to sound like my father."

"Well, maybe I need to talk to him about you being my wife."

"Don't you dare! I will really beat your ass."

"Beat me," he joked as he turned his ass around for me to beat him. I pushed him away from me and began walking out of the hotel room.

"Do you have everything?"

"Yes, Pierre, I do."

We walked to the front of the Hilton hotel and this man pulled up with Pierre's black Lexus, sitting on black rims and black tinted windows. The man jumped out and ran over to me. He took the few bags out of my hand and placed them into the trunk. Pierre put his bags in and we were off. He took me home because I hadn't seen my parents in a while. Plus, my friend Paris came home, but she went to my house, while I spent time with Pierre. She left a voice message letting me know where she was going to be. Paris had caught an early flight. My father was beginning to like Paris a little too much and my mother was worrying me to come home, before she killed him.

Paris came to Mississippi because she was trying to talk me into taking a job at Delicious Divas. I thought about it, but it was too much for me. She should have stayed home in Denver, Colorado. Pierre hated the fact that she was there, because he knew some shit was up. He never liked Paris too much. I don't know why, but he couldn't stand her, and she didn't care too much for him either. He said she looked and dressed like a whore. Pierre was crazy anyway. He hated people because they looked at him wrong.

He had issues.

As we pulled up in the yard, nobody was there. My parents lived next door and even their car was gone. Pierre helped me get my bags out and into the house. The house was very warm and it smelled of a coconut-scented candle. I bought a couple of them when I last shopped. Pierre's cell phone began to ring and he just looked at it.

"Are you going to answer it?"

"Yes, but after I take care of you."

"I'm fine; answer the phone, nigga," I said as I pinched his arm.

"It's Tigga."

"What does he want? Probably a dope deal."

"Girl, stop playing! You know I don't fuck with dope. I'm clean just for your sweet ass. I can't get into any trouble and then not be able to watch you."

"Watch me? You don't need to do that."

"Oh yeah, you mine, baby," he spoke as he wrapped his arms around my waist and started kissing on my neck.

"You better stop that before your dick gets hard."

"Too late, that mutherfucker is up and ready. Bend over for big daddy."

I pulled down my Gucci pants and Victoria Secret panties, and bent over the bed. My pussy was in the air ready to be fucked.

Pierre pulled down his pants and stroked his dick. He licked my pussy from the back and then began to fuck me. I put my head down on the bed as he had his way with me. Pierre stroked my wet, luscious pussy until I came over his dick. When he saw that I had cum, he came in my pussy, leaving his sweet juices behind. He stroked me a few more times and then went into the bathroom. I got off the bed and went behind him. He wiped himself down as I got into the shower.

"Baby, I'm about to call Tigga back, I'll be outside."

"Okay, baby." I looked at him as he straightened his clothes and walked out.

My mind was racing because he was probably fucking one of them chicken heads from South Jackson. They were all after him. They all really thought he was a dope boy. I knew better; his parents would come from the grave to kill his ass. Plus, he wouldn't have me, I don't fuck dope boys.

After I finished my shower, I looked out the window and saw Pierre staring out into space. I knocked on the window and he jumped. I opened my towel and flashed him with my naked body. He smiled and rushed back into the house. I locked my bedroom door so he couldn't get in. He banged on the door until I let him in. We played around for a little while until he received another phone call. This time he wouldn't tell me who it was.

Later, Pierre left to go home and Paris had made it back by

then. My parents had been over and gone home. I thought my dad would never leave, but he took his ass home. My mom was in his ass about Paris. She watched both of them like a hawk; Momma was old but she wasn't a dumb bitch.

Chapter 4

Paris answered her phone while I sat on the couch thinking about all kinds of shit. "Hey baby, what you doing? I can't wait to see your sexy ass again...I know, but I am here in Mississippi on business and will call you when I get back ....Yeah, you're my Peach...Okay, bye."

Hearing the word "Peach", I had to ask to see if it was my Peach, because if it was, there would be hell to pay.

"Who the fuck was that, Paris?" I asked in a mean way.

"My ole girl from Denver, why?"

"You call her Peach, that's the fuck why."

"Bitch, please; you act like you're the only one that can call another bitch Peach."

"Don't make me fuck you up."

"Girl, get off that dumb shit, there are plenty of other names around, and if I call mine Peach, then that's what the fuck I will call her."

"True, but I'm just saying," I said, with a hint of laughter.

"Anyway, Christina, your mother is crazy; I don't want your father."

"Girl, quit fucking with my father."

"I promise I haven't done anything to him, but smile and be friendly."

"Yeah, right. I know how friendly you are," I spoke as I joked with her.

I know she probably played with my father's head, and now he wants some ass. My father has always been a whore, and he will never stop fucking other women. I guess my mother thought she could stop it. She slowed him down, but didn't stop him. I looked at Paris as we sat in the living room and she broke down the cigarillo and rolled up a blunt. I went to the bar in the kitchen and poured up some drinks. She wanted a Long Island Iced Tea, while I fixed me a Vodka Pina Coloda.

Walking over to the window, I had to make sure there was no sign of my parents. I didn't want to be smoking on a blunt and drinking when they busted through the door. My mother always thought she owned my house. Because she was my mom, I allowed her to think that, but sometimes I felt like it's her shit and I just rent a room. I really thought about taking Pierre up on his offer, but he didn't know about my habits, and I sure as hell wasn't ready for him or my parents to find out just how naughty I am.

I glanced back at Paris and said, "Girl, tell me a little more about this job with Delicious Divas."

"Are you sure you want to hear about it? Because I don't want you to be a bad girl," she joked, as she fired up the blunt.

"Bitch, you stupid! Tell me before I change my mind about listening."

"I bring home about $5,000 dollars a week working there. Sometimes, I bring out $10,000 or more. It depends on what I have to do."

"It sounds very interesting, but what all do you have to do?"

Sounding as if she was trying to convince me, she said, "Well, we all attend this party at the home office, and there are men and women standing by, waiting on us to take the stage."

"What stage?" I asked.

"There are nine of us, and we need one more female."

"Stop fucking around and answer the question. What stage?" I asked as she handed me the blunt, and I began to puff and blow.

It's something like a strip club, but we don't dance. We take the stage, and they bid on us."

"Bid?"

"Yes, but the bids start at $1,500 dollars and go up. We put on our best lingerie or costume, and walk the stage like runway. We strut down this walk like models, and they pick who they want by holding up a little paddle with a number on it."

"Bitch, y'all fucking crazy up there in Denver."

"Seriously, you could make up to $5,000 dollars a night, and that's not including the extras you do."

"What do you do? I know there is a catch somewhere. Hit me with the bullshit," I spoke, as I passed the blunt. I downed my drink fast and fixed another one. I sat back down to hear some more shit. Paris had laid back on the couch, like she was buzzed.

"Well, sometimes we fuck the clients that have our number."

"Are you serious, Paris? Sometimes, or all the time, Paris?"

"If you don't fuck, Christina, then the next time you won't get picked by the rich clients. The rich pay a lot more money for a girl. Christina, this is just for one night."

"Bitch, y'all are wild as hell up there in Denver," I said as I puffed again. "And they say us southerners are wild." Taking a sip of my drink, I said, "Shit, Mississippi doesn't have anything on Colorado, even though I have lived up there for two years."

"Christina, you can make mad cash in one night. The rich couples pay more than a single person," Paris said as she puffed the blunt.

"Couples? You mean you fuck men and women?" I had to ask.

With her whorish smile, she said, "Yes, we all do. There are nine of us, four women and five men."

I sat back on my beige-and-chocolate sofa; sipping on the Vodka Pina Coloda I had fixed and listening to Paris run this bullshit down to me. We sat there and smoked the whole blunt. Checking out my friend Paris, I busted out laughing. "Bitch, your pearly-white skin could use a tan."

Laughing at me, she said, "Caramel hoe, don't play, you need to be baked."

That shit she said didn't sound right, but it was funny as hell. Realizing we needed another blunt to simmer down, Paris fixed herself another drink and sat back down to roll another one. It sounded good, but damn.

As the blunt kicked in, my thoughts were more serious and I looked at Paris again. *How her flashing red hair gives way to her green eyes and the body, I would give her a ten.* Then she touched her face and immediately my eyes scanned the pair of small-framed glasses. She favored a school teacher - if you didn't know better, she looked like the nerdy type girl. I further looked over my friend, and she seemed to have her shit together. With her skills and a good game, I rate it as a One. When I put the liquor to my mouth, I pulled my hair to the left and thought, *I would make a good escort. My skin is a flawless caramel and my long black hair is long enough for a woman or man to tug on.* I moved in my seat a

little and my breasts jiggled as I looked down and said, "Oh yeah, breasts and fat juicy ass, you good too, y'all what makes the men and bitches scream 'yeah.'"

Looking down at my legs, I thought, *Pierre loves that shit too. I made the men go crazy the way I strut my ass walking.* Damn, I didn't want to sound desperate, but I wanted the job. My baby Pierre said I didn't have to work, but I didn't get this degree from Nevada State University to be a stay at home chick. All that sounded good, but I want to know more. No, I needed more, because my pussy ached for more.

Paris fired up the blunt and took a couple of puffs. She lay back next to me and relaxed. "Girl, tell me a little bit more about Delicious Divas," I said. "You know that's an undercover whorehouse," I joked.

"Bitch, we are called escorts," she said inside her cup.

"Yeah, right, a legal whorehouse."

We both laughed and smoked the blunt. I had to put down the drinks, because my head was spinning. Paris was used to taking them blunts to the head like that. That bitch did it all, but she was my best friend.

I closed my eyes, sat back, and thought, *Ever since my freshmen year in college, this bitch has hung out with me. The rest of the campus had lame-ass cliques, but Paris, she was Paris - in fact, she was the coolest white girl I ever met.* Smiling, my

thoughts went quickly back to Denver and how they did a lot there, but I wanted to find out about Delicious Divas myself. From the way Paris talked, it was the exact place a bitch like me needed to be.

Pierre had called a couple of times while I was with Paris. He wanted me to come over to be with him, but I wasn't in any condition to do or go anywhere. I just didn't want to hear his shit. Thankfully, the blunts with Paris made me want to take my ass to sleep, but after all that drinking and smoking, I couldn't sleep.

Around two in the morning, I heard some noises and assumed that I had fallen asleep unknowingly, but I was awake. The sounds were heard again and I couldn't make them out; therefore, I laid still and stretched my ears for anything familiar. Tipping out my bedroom door, I saw that the room Paris was sleeping in had a crack in the door. I tiptoed over to it and pushed the door open. The television was playing loud. She wasn't in the bed, so I walked on down the hall. I slowly peeped around the corner into the living room and saw someone over Paris, fucking the shit out of her. I jumped back and started back down the hall. Before I turned to step into the bedroom, they were coming down the hall, so I rushed in my bedroom and pushed the door up. Again, I peeped out to see who she was with, and as if I had seen a ghost, I realized it was my damn father.

That no good bastard! Paris was walking slowly down the hall with a dog collar about her neck. My father was walking behind her with his dick stuck in her, and every step she took he took two, just to make sure he kept her hole plugged. He seemed to be choking her, because in one hand was the dog leash and in the other hand was Paris's ass cheek. I wiped my eyes to make sure of what I saw, but it looks like he whispered something to her, then she turned around and jumped up. He caught her and now he was walking with her down the hall, gripping her ass while fucking her in the air. I put my hand over my mouth to keep from yelling out, "That lying bitch!" She sat there, drinking my liquor, rolling my blunts, sitting on my couch, using my guest room, and that bitch still lied in my damn face -claiming she didn't want my father, and here she is fucking him like he was a young stud! He kept picking her up and popping her on his dick as they went into the bedroom and closed the door. Not believing my eyes, I wanted it to be a dream, but deep down I knew it wasn't. I pushed my door up easily and locked it.

It seemed like my heart was in my panties because I just couldn't believe those two, fucking like it was mating season, while my mom was still in the house next door. Well, I'm sure not going to tell my mother. Fuck that! It hurts, but damn, they grown, and I'm sure Momma knows the dog she had when she came home from the pound. As I laid across my bed, I could hear them. They must have forgotten that I was in the next room, because I could hear her screaming out, "My daddy! I need you!" or "Oh My God,

you're good." What sounded like low grunts was actually my dad, and what really made me put the pillow over my head was when she said, "Shake it in my face or let me drink that nut."

I felt disgusted all over. I know that I do that to my lovers, but to know my dad is getting his dick sucked by a pro made me go to sleep after all.

Chapter 5

"Yes, Mrs. Lee, we are on our way to Denver. We should arrive there around 7 p.m.," Paris spoke to someone on the phone.

Now, Mrs. Lee is the owner of Delicious Divas and the club DLD Ecstasy. She was a very powerful and rich woman. What she wants, she gets. Everyone knew her all around Denver. She had pull in all the places you could only dream of. Everyone knew not to mess with her or her money.

"Come on, Christina," Paris yelled out to me. I was all hugged up with Pierre.

He was begging me not to leave, but money was on my mind. Deep down, he knew I was a real freak. Finally, he let me go, and now we were off to Denver. I know Paris is going to give me the best summer I ever had. This job only pays well during the summertime. The small-timers paid any other day. The rich always had the summers sewed up.

★ ★ ★ ★ ★ 47

We sat back while the plane lifted into the air. I looked at the building, only to see Pierre and my parents look at me taking off. I don't know how I convinced Pierre to let me go. That nigga was always on my ass about leaving him. He felt like Paris was up to something, but he didn't know what. He didn't need to know. I love him to death. When I finish this job, I will go home and marry him. I promised myself that I would be his wife. He loves me so deeply, and the bitches were after him for real.

"I didn't think Pierre would let you go."

"Girl, I told you that I had Pierre. My parents were my problem," I lied.

"You are a woman, not a girl. They weren't going to say anything."

"Yeah, I guess, after you fucked my father."

"Girl, I didn't..."

"Don't play me; I saw the both of you fucking. Girl, my mother would kill me and you. Mainly you for fucking my father, and me for bringing you around the family, you fucking whore," I laughed.

"Bitch, I'm freakier than you think."

"I believe it, too."

"For starters, can I stick my finger in your pussy and taste it?"

I looked at her and stared out the window. She had that very serious look on her face. "Are you fucking serious?"

"Yes, I would love to taste your pussy. I have thought about it for a long time, but didn't know how you would take it."

"So, you are a lesbian now? That was a dumb-ass question, since you say you fuck women too."

"Well, I guess you can say that. It comes with the job. Remember I told you that you have to fuck men and women if you want to make that mad cash."

"I forgot about that part, but I'm down. It's not like I haven't fucked a woman before."

"Bitch, are you for real?"

"Yes, why do you seem so surprised at that?" "No reason," she spoke.

She looked down at my soft caramel legs, as if she was lusting after them. I wore a white flowered dress and six-inch heels. My dress was mid-thigh. Paris looked like she wanted to put her hands down there and see what I would do, but she just asked, "Can I?" she nodded at my skirt.

I continued to stare out the window, and then I slid down in the seat a little and lifted my leg. I didn't look at her, but I knew she would try it anyway. Paris rubbed my thigh up and down, trying to look at the expression on my face. I closed my eyes and laid my head back, but I peeped and she was looking back to see if the people next to us was paying attention. They were fast asleep.

Damn, that was quick for them to be fast asleep, but anyway. I

lifted my leg a little and she stuck her hand on my pussy. As she massaged my clit, for a few seconds I thought, *That shit feels good; I need her to suck that pussy right now.* I didn't want to seem too anxious, but she continued to rub my clit. Paris took her fingers and put them in her mouth with a smile, then stuck her finger down in her own pussy. I was very wet. It didn't surprise me that she didn't open her eyes. She played with that pussy for a while until the flight attendant walked down the aisle and out of sight. Paris then put her hand back between my legs and continued to finger fuck me. It was so funny, because Paris got so wrapped up in doing me, she didn't realize the flight attendant was standing next to her. She turned and looked at her with a nasty look, and she walked off.

"Christina, come go with me."

"Where," I said as I opened my eyes.

"To the bathroom."

"Girl, sit your ass down, I'm not going to the bathroom."

"So I can't taste that pussy?"

"No, just chill."

"I really want to taste that wet mutherfucker," she whispered while tasting her finger.

I continued to just stare out the window, so she left me alone about the whole situation. But she did get a chance to stick her fingers in that pussy again and taste my juices off her fingers. I

laughed at Paris, because she thought she was crazy. She wasn't crazy; she just wanted to taste this honey.

It came over the intercom to fasten the seatbelts and that we were about to land in Denver, Colorado. We strapped down and landed. Mrs. Lee was probably going to be at the airport herself. Mrs. Lee was anxious to see me again. She saw me one summer when I came to visit Paris at the club, and ever since then she wanted me back. I wouldn't be surprised if she wanted to do me. Then again, she wanted the best.

"Finally, I am home!" Paris yelled out.

"Girl, I'm really beginning to believe that you are wild."

"You haven't seen nothing yet. Look, there is our ride over there," Paris spoke.

We walked over to Mrs. Lee's black Mercedes Benz. Felix, the driver, opened up the door, and we jumped in. "Hello Ms. Christina, how was your ride?" Mrs. Lee asked.

"It was as boring as I thought it was going to be."

"Did Paris explain everything to you about Delicious Divas?"

"No, not everything. There are a few minor details that I forgot to mention," Paris jumped in.

"Well Paris, I see you are not on your job like I thought you would be. Were you too busy tasting the product, or what? Here is your bonus," she stated.

When Mrs. Lee handed her that big hunk of cash, my eyes didn't blink or anything.

"What's that for?" I asked.

"That's Paris's money for recruiting you," Mrs. Lee spoke.

I looked at Paris as if I could have put my foot off in her ass. She failed to mention about how she was getting a bonus for me. It's too late now, I'm in the game. Mrs. Lee explained everything to me, about what she expected and didn't expect. Mrs. Lee was very strict when it came to her girls, but they all broke the rules here and there. If she knew, she would probably shit bricks.

"Paris, you will take Christina to the Eldora Inn Suites and get her ready to go see Dr. Bonita. Make sure that everything is in place, because tomorrow night is the grand opening for us."

"Yes ma'am, Christina will be ready," Paris spoke.

"Why am I staying at a hotel?" I asked, before Mrs. Lee exited the vehicle.

"Because I want you to be ready, with no distractions. I know you have an apartment over there off Chestnut Drive. I want your mind to be focused on what needs to be done. We could make millions this summer. I have new clients coming from all over the world," she explained.

Mrs. Lee exited the car. I wanted to go off on Paris, but I just sat back and rode to the hotel. When I got a break, I would call Peaches and Pete to let them know I was back in town. But first, I

was going to call my baby. I called Pierre, but he didn't answer his phone. I called six times in a row and the mutherfucker didn't answer. I'm going to dig all in his ass when he does call me back.

Chapter 6

We arrived at the doctor's office, and I didn't know what to expect. Paris was being all hush-hush about the shit. Mrs. Lee was the head woman, and Paris acted like her right-hand man. I sat in the medium-sized office looking at the white walls with all types of colorful pictures, when the doctor entered the room.

"Hello, Ms. De'Angelo, how are you doing today?"

"I'm good for right now."

"I see that you work for Delicious Divas and that you need a full-body checkup."

"Yes ma'am, I do. I don't see why, but I do."

She looked at me very puzzled and began to put little instruments together on the table. A nurse came in to help her with everything, and then I saw the materials. Honestly, I didn't know

what to expect, but either way, I knew it would be a clean bill of health.

"Ms. De'Angelo, I'm going to need you to take all your clothes off and put this on. Make sure you have it open in the front."

"Okay."

They both left the room while I stripped down. *This must be required*, I thought as I took off all my clothes and put them away neatly. Then it hit me. Mrs. Lee was getting me ready to fuck. Now I remember that Paris told me that first-timers made big money; therefore, I planned to live the high life without Pierre's money, even though he wanted me to be his wife so badly. I loved that nigga, but I didn't want his money, only his love.

Dr. Bonita came back in with the nurse. I lay out on the table waiting for her to check me. To my surprise, she said, "I need you to get off the table and bend over."

"Okay," I replied, but I thought, *How unusual for a patient to get off the table for an examination.*

I bent over and she ruffled up the paper pullover dress I had on. She pushed my left leg, motioning me to spread my legs wider. I touched my toes and spread my legs wide, leaving my pussy open for anything. Dr. Bonita placed her small hand on my back and asked, "Do you feel my hand?" as she began rubbing my clit.

"Yes, I feel your hand on my clit," I spoke in a low tone. as she turned me on.

"May I enter you? You are so wet and smell so sweet," Dr. Bonita spoke.

Not knowing what to think, I could only reply, "Yes, yes, Dr. Bonita, do as you please."

Dr. Bonita stuck her index finger in my pussy, and moved in and out. I stood up straight, to see that the nurse was standing and guarding the door. She was looking as if she was ready to taste my sweet pussy.

"I need you to get up on the table. I have to taste this dripping-wet pussy," she spoke.

I got up on the table and put my feet in the stirrups, sliding down to the edge of the table. The nurse locked the door and walked over to us. Dr. Bonita began rubbing my inner thighs, then with her fat tongue she began tasting my pussy, while the nurse opened the paper dress and tenderly sucked on my breasts one at a time. I became so aroused by the two women taking my body like no other, my mind started a whirlwind of thoughts: *Is this shit really real? Have I ever had two women? Hell no, only one at a time! However, these some smart-ass freaky bitches.* Interrupting my thoughts, I decided to take my hand off the table to rub between the nurse's legs, and she had no panties on. I found her moist pussy and began playing with her clit, as she made low moaning noises. After sucking on my clit, Dr. Bonita was tongue fucking me and I liked that shit. In fact, she was better than

Peaches. Damn, these females had a bitch going crazy. They have me ready to be down for whatever they could bring.

The nurse grinded on my fingers for a few extra minutes before she stepped away from the table to enter this small closet. I was speechless, because she came out with a pink-and-black strap-on dick. I looked between my legs and Dr. Bonita stopped tongue-fucking me to pull off her doctor's coat, and she too was butt fucking naked. I'm beginning to wonder, *Is this really a doctor's office? These bitches have no clothes on and have a closet with toys ready to fuck. Oh hell no, this can't be the doctor's office.*

I liked the way her breasts looked, so I waved for her to come closer, and she did. As she leaned closer, the dangling breast was plump and the nipple fit perfectly into my mouth. She gave me one breast then the other, while the nurse squeezed her own breasts with excitement. Dr. Bonita moved away from me to put on the strap-on dick. When she stepped on the low stool, she pulled me further down on the table then slowly, she entered me with the huge-sized, firm cock. Wanting to join the fun, the nurse climbed on top of the table and straddled me, placing her ass to me with her pussy open. I looked at her almost worn-out pussy and stuck my tongue out on her long clit.

Each time the good doctor would enter me hard, the nurse would suck my clit and rise up as if she was doing an exercise move. Getting my mind back on pleasing her, I looked at her

rough-looking pussy, but once my tongue dipped into the sticky treat, the shit tasted sweet. When the nurse tried to get up, I would hold her to my face, and with each upward move, I would throw my pussy to the doctor. The nurse placed her arms around the doctor and began kissing her, while I tried to drink her up, but the doctor was winning. She was making my pussy cum over and over again, nothing big, but enough to release a little built-up pressure. The nurse let go of the doctor. She was putting that pussy on my face harder, and I was taking full advantage of making her reach her peak. I would suck, lick and pull on her pussy with everything, because I never back down from a challenge. However, I was not ready for the nurse to release, so I stopped for her to get up.

The nurse got off my face and the doctor stopped fucking me. They changed positions and the doctor's pussy looked like a virgin's. When she sat down on my face, I fell in love. I didn't have to lift a thing; that pussy sat right there. "This pussy is right here for you; eat that bitch up," the doctor said, and I quickly got crunk by licking and sucking on that clit. Immediately she was warm as her juices flowed into my mouth like raindrops, but I didn't stop. She told me to eat this bitch up, and I intended to make her run for help.

The more emphasis I placed on that clit and the more I sucked on the pussy lips, the more hysterical her movement became. In stride, I would take my tongue 'round and 'round on that clit and

work my way to the bottom of it. It made the good doctor's pussy bulge, and just like that she came on my face. I wanted to choke because it tasted like hell, but I continued to lick that nasty mutherfuckering pussy, and being a real freak, I put my face all in it. After that orgasm, she rode my face slow, and believe me, I tried to go as deep as I could. But on the other hand, the strap-on the nurse had was taking me slow then a little faster, slow then a little faster. *She's getting carried away*, I thought as she would take it out slow and shove it back in faster. *If I was a weak bitch, that shit would have my mind blown. They want a freak, and they got a freak*, I thought.

The doctor switched around and started sucking on my breasts, while the nurse fucked me and licked on the doctor. With flicks of her tongue on my nipples, they hardened, and I would moan loudly enough for her to hear. She kissed on the entire breast, and each time my nipple was in her mouth, she would bite down teasingly. The excitement sent chills throughout my body. At one point, she smothered her face into my luscious mounds and licked her way out, and the tingling sensation felt wonderfully good.

After a lot of licking, sucking, and fucking, things ended. They put on their clothes as if nothing had happened. All I could do was smile, because I never thought that getting a checkup would be so much damn fun. While I got dressed, another nurse came back in and took me to a bathroom. "Dr. Bonita says you need to clean up before you leave the office," she instructed.

"Okay ma'am. What am I supposed to clean up with?" I spoke.

"Look to your left. There are a few towels over there with soap." She walked out like she had an attitude. She must not know I will get in her ass. I will show her how we beat a bitch's ass in Mississippi! I don't like bitches like that. Don't hate; get like me.

After I cleaned up, I walked back to the front with Paris. She had a big-ass grin on her face.

"Bitch, you look tired," she spoke sarcastically.

"I'm a little tired. You didn't tell me they were going to fuck me, and on top of that, double-team me."

"Double team. Who?"

"Dr. Bonita and the nurse both fucked and licked my sweet-ass pussy."

"Damn Christina, I'm surprised the doctor got down with you," she spoke.

"Bitch, why you say it like that? You sound like I'm nasty and shit."

"No bitch, I was just saying that the doctor never tastes the patients. Especially Dr. Bonita; she is picky about who she goes down on."

"Well Paris, that lets me know I have that powerful shit. My pussy is the bomb!"

"Bitch, she probably went down on you because your pussy looks like nobody had ever touched it."

"Stop hating."

"I'm not hating, bitch, I'm for real," she spoke as we walked outside and entered a limousine.

"Hello again, Christina. How was your doctor's visit?" Mrs. Lee asked with a big smile.

"It was very different, but I liked my treatment. They both were good."

"Both."

"Yes, Dr. Bonita and the nurse gave me a treat," I spoke.

"Okay, cool. So Jennie was involved?" she asked.

"Who?"

"Dr. Bonita. She was involved as well?"

"Yes ma'am, she was, and damn it was good," I expressed.

"Good. You must have some fire pussy. Well, before this summer ends and you rush back off to Mississippi, I want you to come to my house for the weekend with me and my husband," she stated.

"Sounds good to me."

"But, you have never - " Paris began to say, but cut it off.

"I never what?" Mrs. Lee asked her. Paris just shook her head and leaned back in the car. I knew what she was about to ask, and so did Mrs. Lee. Paris sat back with this sad-ass look on her face. I

just hope I didn't have to beat this bitch down before the summer was over with. Focusing back on the boss lady, my mind wondered, *What else hasn't she done with Mrs. Lee?*

Chapter 7

Mrs. Lee dropped us off in front of the club and dipped. She didn't say shit. Paris took me inside the club. I was looking around like a newbie, hoping it didn't show on my face. To the left when you first walked in, there was a small booth where the attendant sat to the take the money. As I walked on down the narrow hallway, there were different naked pictures of men and women, leading down to these two big doors. Paris opened one door and the room was sparkling. You would think it was a fucking rundown place until you saw this.

"Wow, Paris, this is so beautiful," I spoke.

"Well, there is the stage we have to walk. The bar is over there to your left. The dressing room is in the back of the stage," she explained.

"Do the people sit out here?"

"They are called clients, and yes, they do sit out here. The highest-paid high rollers always sit in the front. They get first dibs at you."

"Okay, but I thought they would, only if, they would have our number?" I asked, confused.

"I did say that before, but no; they bid on you. Say you walk out on the stage and model for them. The bid starts at $1,500 dollars and goes higher. If the client or clients want to pay high dollars for you, they will keep bidding until the lower ones back down," she explained.

"Okay, I see. Well, how do we get paid, because I know the money doesn't come to us directly?" I asked.

"No, it doesn't. The split is 60/40. Mrs. Lee and the club gets 60%."

"Damn, that's not enough."

"You will see what I'm talking about once you get started."

We walked around some more, as she showed me different spots. They had a room where the swingers could get down. A lot of couples paid good money just to get in. Not just anyone could enter; you had to pay. Paris took me backstage and introduced me to NeNe, Cherry, and Chocolate. Then she took me to the men and introduced me to Nutt Butter, Stud, Sweet Ass, Candy Strip, and Pink Pussy. The mutherfuckers were too damn fine, but they all wanted the same thing I was after: dick. Paris introduced me to the

bartenders, the bouncer, and of course, Mr. Lee. He was finer than Wesley Snipes's chocolate ass. Damn!

Paris's cell rung and it was Mrs. Lee. She stepped away like it was some big secret. The bitch was beginning to be a little suspicious, if you ask me. She had become a whole different person ever since I talked to Mrs. Lee. This bitch was really ill.

"Well, it looks like you won't be performing tonight, Ms. Christina De'Angelo," she spoke with a happy tone.

"Why is that?" I asked.

"Because Mrs. Lee stated that she will have you doing the opening act next week. She wants to advertise you first, and then put you out there. Basically, you are new meat, and the money could really roll in. She's expecting to make at least 100K off you."

"Bitch, stop lying. 100K is a lot of money."

"I'm serious as a monkey loving bananas."

"What you just said sounded so dumb."

"Anyway, I'm going to show you the ropes and then turn you lose. You might cramp my style, and I might start losing money fucking off with you. Nobody wants to be with the newcomer, and since you are my friend, I'm stuck with you," she spoke.

"Bitch, you say you are stuck with me. What kind of fucking friend are you? Don't tell me you one of those fake ass bitches that

pretend to be your friend one minute and your enemy the next? Damn bitch, didn't know you were like that," I snapped.

"Bitch, don't play with me. You will always be my friend. I didn't mean it like that."

"Yeah, but that's the way I took it," I snapped back.

"Stop being so damn sensitive at times. Damn!"

Paris walked off and left me standing there looking stupid. I walked over to the bar and sat down. I wanted to pick up one of those bottles and smash that bitch in the head. She was really beginning to piss me off. "What the fuck has gotten into her?"

I felt my cell phone vibrate; it was Pierre calling me back. I rushed out the door because I didn't want him to hear the loud music. Closing the door, I answered, but he hung up. I called his ass back and he picked up on the first ring.

"Run your mouth," he spoke.

"Where the fuck have you been, nigga? I've been blowing up that raggedy-ass phone, and you didn't answer. What's up with that?"

"Baby, calm down, I had an important business meeting and couldn't pick up the phone."

"Don't fuck with me, Pierre! Are you trying to play these mind games?"

"Baby girl, you know I fucking love you. Don't even try to play me as one of them weak-ass mutherfuckers. What the fuck you was doing when I called just now?" he asked.

"I was trying to answer my phone. It was in my purse."

"Yeah, I see."

"Boy, don't play with me like that," I stated.

"Okay, what did you want?" he asked.

"Nothing but this, Pierre," I spoke as I hung up the phone in his face. Fuck him; he's not all that important.

I began to walk back into the club and my phone was going off. Pierre was calling me back-to-back. I'm not fucking off with this nigga today. He wants to play pussy. Okay, cool. Play pussy and get fucked. That's what will happen, and he knows this.

A few minutes later, Paris and I left to go back to the hotel. She dropped me off and headed back to the club. I'm not staying in this mutherfucker all night by myself. I called up Pete and Peaches, trying to see if they would come downtown and fuck. Peaches had the kids and Pete was nowhere to be found. Lately, I noticed that Peaches had been alone. I hope they were doing all right.

To ease my mind off Pete, Peaches and Pierre, I decided to go for a swim in the heated pool to relax my mind. When I got there, a couple was playing in the water. *How cute they looked together*, I thought. When the door closed, a sign read "Do not close, door will lock." *Too late; someone will be around shortly, just hope they don't get mad.*

I turned my attention back to the couple in the pool. He had his back on the edge while she was in front of him, kissing him on his neck. So as not to invade their privacy, I went to the other end dropping my towel to reveal my two-piece suit. He smiled, but I paid them no more attention, until she stopped pleasing her man, to bid me to come over to them.

"Hey, my name is Share and this is my brother Jon, what's yours?"

Oh hell no, did this bitch say brother? It blew my mind and I gagged in front of them, because earlier, I wouldn't have thought that at all.

"Don't look like that?" she said. "You act like family dick, isn't the best dick. Think about it. No one would suspect it, and if it's good dick like his is…" She licked her lips and continued, "You'll do what you have to do to get that nut."

"Well, if you like it, I love it," I said with a smile. "By the way, the name's Christina, nice to meet you both."

"Christina, I recognize my type - I mean a freak, that is. Want to play with us?"

It was late and there was nothing to do, so I told her, "I'll tell you what. I'll watch, and if it is a good movie, I'll play."

Her brother Jon got out of the water, placed his hands flat on the surface, and sat with his feet hanging in. He had a huge cock and it leaned with a crook. His top was ripe and it shone like no other. *If he knows how to use it, I can see why that incest bitch was sneaking off to get it*, I thought as I swam closer to get a personal view. Share put her entire mouth on his shaft. Jon had to be at least ten inches, and she swallowed every bit. Her lips were the only thing brushing against his nut sack, and when she gripped the dick with her mouth, she smacked her lips as she came off him. Looking at his dick, I saw that it stood higher and harder than before. *This bitch won't outdo me*, I said to myself. She was licking all the water off that strong-ass dick, and I could tell she was enjoying it. Share took one of her hands and massaged his sack and said, "How many you think I can get out of here tonight?"

He replied, "Get as many as you can, but save some for her."

At that moment, he scooted a little farther back so his feet could hang over the water. Share started licking from his ass to the top of his dick, and every so often she would thump it. Each time she took his swollen manhood into her mouth, he would moan a little louder. She proceeded to take his sack into her mouth and pulled his balls slightly back and forth, likc a tug-of-war game. Then she licked up and down his pole from every angle, and when she got to the top, she kept his mushroom cap in her mouth and used her tongue to play with it. He snatched her head and pushed

himself deeper into her mouth. Seconds later, Jon let go of her head and started hitting the floor with his palms. Share looked at me, and only some of his juices were on her lips, because she swallowed the rest. I looked at his dick, and it was slimy but still standing strong. Share saw me admiring it and she licked that dick clean. When she got all his juices off the dick, she kissed the head. She turned to me and said, "Tag, you're it!"

Aw, this is a bad incest bitch! How the hell can I top off that? I thought. When I turned to Jon, he was sitting again with his feet in the water while Share was close by. Placing my arms under Jon's thighs, I told him to lift his hands up in the air, and when he did, I pulled him into the water and squared my legs to hold us up while his legs hung over my shoulders. At that moment, I began to taste his full nut sack. Thankfully, the water came up to my neck, and that allowed me enough room to only move my head. I began to suck and tease his sack with my tongue and he began to shake a little. I could only go so far up the stem because his dick was long, but that did not stop me from using what I could.

With every suck and tug I did on his sack, he jumped and played in my hair. From behind, I felt Share playing in my pussy with her fingers, and then she went underwater and sucked my clit. Every minute she would come up for air, and then go down on me again. I was beginning to tremble, because it was very kinky to have my pussy nibbled at underwater. This time when she came up, I walked Jon over to the edge, because I had to taste that dick and possibly drink that nut better than his sister. When Jon sat his bottom on the edge, he went all the way back with his feet completely out of the water.

The pleasure became mine as I got the chance to taste the stick that had been staring me in the face. I allowed my feet to hang on the edge of the pool, while I eagerly slid my mouth on him. It wouldn't fit, so I forced it and nearly choked, but how sexy it felt to have a huge cock hanging out of my mouth. Numerous times, I would grip my mouth on him and pull upwards, having my tongue play with him for a few minutes. Share was watching me give joy to her brother, and she came over and stood between my legs in the pool, and licked my pussy to my ass. Her tongue distracted me from being delighted with Jon's dick, because her tongue went deep inside my ass. I could only give him a nice hand job, because his sister was driving me in-fucking-sane. Share began to roll her tongue around in my ass and she blew a lot of warm air into it and that made my big ass wiggle.

Share began to smack my ass and she said, "This is my ass, Christina; it belongs to me, not Jon." Then she pulled on my legs so they could hang on her shoulders straight, and when she put her mouth on my pussy from this position, my pussy juices went all over her lips and nose.

I couldn't stop having multiple orgasms. When the first one came, she stopped licking me. When that one went away, she started again, and I filled her mouth up with my liquid nut. I could feel her sucking on my pussy lips, trying to get all the juice off them. She sucked more and more, and with each sucking, it became more intense than the last sucking. She finally moved, and I was unsure I could move my legs; therefore, I used my elbows to slide up to Jon, and amazingly, he was still hard as a rock.

Share sat on his face and we both sucked on him. When cum started to roll down the sides of his dick, we both were being greedy; trying to see who could lick the most cum up. Then Share left the dick to me, and she was humping Jon's face and squeezing her breasts. He was limp now. Therefore, while Jon was still lying there, I got behind Share and licked her ass. It smelled of cinnamon and oranges. The more I smelled her, the more I tried to wrap her ass around my face. Jon was eating the pussy and I was tongue-fucking her ass. Finally, Share began to do short hard grinding on him, but I lifted her ass up and drank the nut. I began to pull on her pussy lips and taste her, but I did it better, because she was begging me to stop and I wouldn't. I had to show off. Share came again twice more in my mouth, and it was more than the last time.

"Please stop, please stop, Christina. I know it is you!" she cried out, but I just couldn't. I had to take her a little higher. I told her to suck the dick and shut up. Share complied with my instructions,

and Jon got hard again. When I moved out of the way, Jon picked up where I left off by licking the pussy and tongue-fucking her. I looked up, and Share was sucking that dick like it was the last, but I had to sit on it, just to see if I could take the ten inches. I pulled her up and put my pussy on the dick, and not surprisingly, the pussy sucked up the balls too. It felt good, and I could feel every inch of him. Slowly, I began to ride him, and he would try to push his dick up, but I would grind a little bit slower to drive him crazy.

Whenever he would try to throw it back, I said, "Did I tell you to move? Then be still." Share's pussy was in his mouth and he couldn't talk back, but I had to let him know who was in charge on that dick of his. After a few more grinding sessions he tensed up, and I knew what that meant, so I got up and let the high-powered cum shoot all over my face. Then I slapped his dick all around my face, and in and out of my mouth. Before he could get soft, I licked up all the juice, mines and his, because I don't like to leave evidence. By chance, I looked up, and Share had quit enjoying herself and was watching the way I took care of her brother. She got angry and got up. When she moved out of the way, I put my pussy in his face.

Not taking my eyes off hers, I began to lick the huge dick her brother has, and when that didn't finish making her mad, I took my teeth and nibbled at it. This caused Jon's toes to curl and spread. She stormed to the other side of the pool and I laughed, because

she needed to know that whenever I fuck off, I'm the damn queen not the servant. Before that thought was finished, Jon was drinking from my pussy fountain, and after that, I was completely out of juice. Slowly I got up, and Jon whispered to me, "Christina, you give fire-ass head, but don't tell Share that. When can we have our own private meeting?"

I replied, "Sorry, I am booked, but it was fun." I got up and put on my bathing suit, and before the pool attendant opened the door, I said, "It was great, you guys, especially you, Share." I winked at her, went to my room, bathed and fell asleep.

Chapter 8

It was Tuesday, and it was boring as fuck. Mrs. Lee wanted me to stay in the fucking hotel all week because she wanted my pussy to be fresh. At first, I disagreed until she paid me $1,000 to sit my ass down. My pussy was throbbing and I needed some dick attention, or a bitch to lick this pussy again. She didn't know that I don't give out. I love to fuck, suck and lick clit, I don't get tired, and my pussy is better every time I am in a sex meeting. However, she didn't want any type of sexual acts going on. I started thinking about how badly I needed to be penetrated. I walked over to my desk and picked out the long, bumpy, pink dildo and thought, *She didn't say I couldn't have a little me time.* I began to caress my secret friend, so he could earn his place in my desk, but thought, *Why not add something healthy? It has been a while since I played "who can go the farthest".* I walked over to the phone and my

fingers dialed for room service. All I had to do was wait on the knock.

When the servant finally arrived, I was hotter than before. I thought about giving him some, but human dick was not on my mind. Therefore, I gave him a tip and closed the door immediately. Walking back to the portable table, I took the top off the food and swiftly admired the cucumbers, green bananas, strawberries, and peeled oranges. Licking my lips, I tasted a strawberry and smiled with fresh thoughts of, *What fruity moments I am about to have,* as my pulse raced with anticipation of inserting the huge, good-smelling cucumbers, deep within me.

Rolling the cart over to the six-foot-long coffee table, I cleared the magazines, sat on the table, and placed the cart between my legs. Smearing my breasts with the oranges' juice, I closed my eyes and began moving my body to the rhythm in my head. Turning my nipple up towards me, I started sucking the tangy-tasting juice on my body. Removing my mouth, I ate a few strawberries and began tasting my breasts again - *how sweet* - as my nipple rolled around in my mouth. Having spent enough time on my breasts, I grabbed the biggest cucumber with my right hand and felt around, until I had the hardest, longest and greenest unpeeled banana with my left hand. Lying on the coffee table on my back, I inserted the cucumber deep within my pussy walls. My body began to slow dance to the music the cucumber played, as it

penetrated me. Opening my mouth, I started sucking the banana in tune with the cucumber, taking the fruits deep inside both at one time, feeling pleasure and bliss as I did.

The faster I pulled on the banana, the harder and deeper my hand thrust the cucumber within me. Not able to take the fruit arousal, I pulled the fruit away and shook for a few seconds. As my eyes opened, I placed the cucumber in my mouth and thought, *Enough with the play fun.* So I got off the table, picked up my space-keeping friend, and stepped into the bath water. Enjoying the water upon my skin, I placed my right leg out of the water and lay there, as my hand held my friend in place, while it sent chills between my legs. Thinking, *I love the feel of the dick vibrating inside of me*, I let it relax me so much, I thought I would die from being over-pleased. Smiling at the thought of being found in a hotel room with a huge vibrating cock between my legs was funny, and I laughed.

Feeling refreshed, I pulled my friend from under the water, stood up and kissed him, for he has earned his keep tonight. As I dried off, I put my pleasure stick up and went to sleep.

Days passed by and Friday was finally here. I was to appear at the club at seven o' clock sharp. There was this VIP section with a big-ass pink-and-gold chair up on a stage. It was on the side of the club. Mrs. Lee gave me a red and white candy striper outfit to put on with red boots that came up to my knees. The thongs were red

and of course, no bra. You know my big-ass tits were about to pop out of that too-small shirt. My hair was combed into two long ponytails, like a little elementary kid. She sent a lady over that day to give me a manicure and pedicure. I soaked in milk and honey, for that gloss on my already pretty golden-brown skin.

The limo pulled up at the door and I stepped into the building like I was the shit. As soon as I walked in, I noticed that the club was empty. I'm looking around, like why in the hell am I here so early, only to come to a naked-ass room. Straightening up my walk, I went to the back office to find Mrs. Lee.

"Hello, Christina. I'm glad you are here on time."

"Where are the people?" I asked.

"They will be here at eight. I needed you here early to make sure you are looking like a million bucks. These people are going to pay big money once they see you tonight."

"I'm going on stage tonight?" I asked excitedly.

"Hell no, not tonight, but you will go on tomorrow. I just want to advertise you tonight for the guests."

"Okay, sounds good to me."

"Come over here and let me taste that pussy, before the clients start coming in."

I didn't say a word; I just walked over to her desk. Mr. Lee was standing back looking at us and one of the bodyguards.

"Bend over my desk and spread those legs wide," she demanded.

I did as she told me. She pulled my thong to the side and sniffed my pussy. "Damn, this shit smell so good. She got that virgin-looking pussy," she spoke. After sniffing, she ran her tongue tenderly between my pussy lips; giving me chills all over. She licked and licked for a few seconds, and sucked on the clit. She felt me wiggle a little. "Mr. Lee, come over and get you a taste of this good shit," she spoke to her husband, while tasting me more before he came.

Quickly, he rushed over like a little kid and ran his big lips over my pussy. I could have cum in his fucking face. I could tell that his tongue was wide and greedy. It seemed like he tried to swallow my pussy whole. His mouth was big enough to cover me, and I could literally feel him sucking my pussy up, like he was sucking water out of a sponge. He would take that big tongue of his and flap it up and down my pussy as a teaser, than sucked on my clit. He was getting pleasure watching my pussy bulge for him. Mrs. Lee moved him out of the way and began tasting me with perfection. They were taking turns licking me from the back. I stood there straddling the desk, enjoying every moment the pair was giving me. I looked up at the bodyguard and his dick was rock hard. He wanted to taste the fucking pussy too. I licked my lips at him, and moved my finger in and out of my mouth, just for him to see.

After they finished, Mrs. Lee took some type of soft towel and wiped me down good. She wanted all the moistness to be gone. She wanted me to look fresh before the buzzards got here. Straightening up my clothes, she spoke, "This will be your new bodyguard. His name is Dave. He will be with you tonight. Anytime you go to a client's house that we do not know, he will be the one to take you there and bring you back home."

"Someone you don't know. So they are not the regular clients?" I asked.

"Some are old and some new, but they all have big money. Do you understand what I'm talking about?" she spoke while shaking her head up and down. I looked at her, shaking my head up and down right along with her as she continued, "Great, I'm glad we have good communication. But before you walk out, I have to cover you with this gold glitter."

"Gold glitter?"

"Yes, it will have your body sparkling over your golden brown skin," she spoke.

"Sure," I spoke, and I stood posted against her desk with my legs spread wide.

She began rubbing me all over with this gold glitter. It really did make my body sparkle, especially when we walked out into the

crowd and the white neon lights shone down upon me. It wasn't packed, but there were enough people for me to grab everyone's attention. I began strutting down the aisle like a stallion, throttling for a contest.

As I showed off, I could see Mr. And Mrs. Lee looking down at me from the upper VIP section. Dave followed me to the lower part of the VIP section, which was decorated with gold and white balloons. Streamers hung from the ceiling. As I stepped up onto the stage, there was a huge table decorated with fruits. I saw kiwis, tangerines, pineapples, strawberries, peaches, grapes, oranges and red and gold apples. My mind was racing. What the hell is this all about? The people from the crowd were staring at me and I was looking back at them.

"Christina, you have to strip naked and lay on the table in the middle of the fruit," spoke Dave.

"Are you for real? While all these people staring at me?" I asked.

"Yes, you have to put on a show. The more you show, the more money they will offer to take you home. I will protect you. The more you get paid, the more I get paid," he smiled.

"Okay, cool. I don't mind giving these ladies and gentlemen a show."

I looked up at Mrs. Lee and she began to smile, showing nothing but teeth. Mr. Lee nodded his head as if telling me to go

ahead and strip. Turning towards the crowd, I removed my shirt and threw it into the crowd. They were acting wild as I shook my breasts. I turned around and shook my ass, then turned around so they could see me rubbing my nipples and licking them with my long tongue. The crowd liked that a lot, because I heard someone say, "I'll buy your ass tonight!" Afterwards, I took off my thong and exposed my big, beautiful ass. My cheeks began to slap together, making slapping noises, then I let my ass jiggle one cheek at a time.

Bending over and spreading my legs, I stuck my fingers in my pussy, playing around. I took my fingers out and tasted my honey. Dave waved for me to get up on the table. I walked over to the table covered in fruit; Dave lifted me up and placed me in the middle. As soon as I lay back, two big poles from the floor began to rise. I watched as they stood high with strings hanging from them. Dave took my legs and placed them in stirrups like at a doctor's office. I slid down to the edge so my calf would rest flat. After tying my legs down, he tied each arm down and then placed a small band across my head to pin me down. My heart began to skip a beat as I wondered what the fuck was really about to go on.

I didn't recall signing up to be tied down with ropes and shit. Dave moved back, and two Chinese ladies rushed over and began preparing the fruits around me like I was dinner. Fruits were all around me. I had to lie still as the show began. The music began to

play and I wanted to turn my head to see what the hell was going on, but my head was pinned down. Listening to the crowd, they began to cheer like men at a strip club. The announcer came on introducing Ms. Chocolate. You could hear more women cheering than men. But the men were there, and my pussy started jumping.

Things came to my mind about me getting up on stage. I want to turn that mutherfucker out, once I get up there. I have to stand out from the rest of the females. Ms. Chocolate and Ms. Nene were built like stallions. These two bitches were so fine. I wanted to taste the bitches myself. Lying there on the table waiting, impatiently, I began to fidget.

"Ms. Christina, you have to be still," one of the ladies said as she gave me this nasty look.

"Yeah, you be still," the other lady spoke, while pushing my legs back down.

I wanted to get up and break my foot off in their asses. My pussy was exposed and dripping. Shit, this wasn't what I expected. I needed someone to be licking or sucking on my clit, or possibly fucking me. Maybe Mrs. Lee and her husband could come down and give me what I'm wishing for. I looked up at them, and they stared out into the crowd, looking at Ms. Chocolate take the stage. The announcer was going on and on like one of those men at an auction, trying to sell some expensive shit. Finally, he got up to $6,000 dollars and stopped.

More girls walked on stage, one after the other and got picked. After things died down and the four girls were picked, the rest of the crowd stood around mingling like some buzzards. Many walked over looking over at me, as if they were ready to take me home.

The announcer got on the intercom and announced, "Ladies and gentlemen, it is time for happy hour." Everyone began slapping their hands. The two women moved me down closer to the edge of the table and began fixing the fruit. One of the women walked away and returned with a bowl of fruit. She began to pour this slimy bowl of fruit all over me. It looked like it was mixed with some type of cocktail juice. That shit was cold on my skin and making chills stand up all over my body, and my nipples rose. "It's time for round one. For the ones who are not participating, please be seated until it is time for round two," the announcer spoke.

"Time for what?" I asked the lady.

With a smile she replied, "It's time for them to eat you out; they are going to taste you. Each person has five minutes to taste you, before the next one comes up."

"Are you serious?" I asked her.

"Yes, I'm for real, lady," she spoke.

In my ears was Lil Wayne singing "Dick Pleaser", and that shit pushed away all my doubts and caused my body to come alive. I could feel people entering the stage. I was trying to look down

below, and I saw a dark-skinned woman with dreads, bending down and looking at my pussy. She began to taste me. Her tongue slid down my clit so slowly. She sucked my clit kind of hard then released me. I began moving my hands around, wanting to grab her head and ram it deeper within me, but I couldn't. She licked and licked until I got ready to cum, then she stopped. Damn, I wanted to get that nut off. She walked off stage and then this big, fat, caramel-colored brotha stepped up. He was at least three hundred pounds. He licked out his tongue at me. Damn, he had a fat ass tongue. He got down and I thought he swallowed my pussy whole. He licked and licked me. Every time I got ready to nut in someone's mouth, they stopped eating this pussy. Damn.

There were around ten people that had tasted me. All their tongues felt so damn good, except for one guy. He needed some more pussy-eating lessons. I knew I felt teeth on me. After all the taste testing, the announcer got back on the microphone. "Who's ready for round two? You all need to get your partner. The numbers that you received at the beginning of the show, you will line up in that order. Some of you will have the same number. If so, then that is your partner for round two." He continued, "If you do not have a partner, one will be given to you. Who doesn't have a partner?"

I guess nobody raised their hands, because he continued, "Let the party began."

I was trying to look around, and one of the women loosened the strap across my head so I could move. I looked to my left and saw these people standing there naked. Some were still pulling off clothes.

"Dave, what's going on man?" I asked in a little fear.

"Oh baby, just chill. They're going to see how good your pussy is before they offer big bucks."

"What you mean by that? They all going to fuck me at one time?" I asked.

"It will be two at a time and they only have three minutes. They will fuck you until the music stops then they will change up. The bid is already up to thirty thousand dollars."

"You have got to be fucking kidding me," I said with a chuckle.

"No baby, I'm not kidding," he replied.

As I was being presented for tasting and short thrills, I did not know what to expect. The announcer said, "Here's a little something to help happy hour along." Then I heard Luke Skywalker singing "Head, Booty and Cock." The sexual lyrics aroused me, as they eased my mind. Suddenly, two guys entered the stage. One walked up to me and began putting dick in my pussy. I let out a low sigh. He wasn't that big. This other guy stepped up to the table and put his dick straight in my mouth. He held my head to the side and began stroking. I sucked him slowly.

This other guy was trying to fuck me good in those three minutes. The music stopped and they switched out. The small dick guy approached me and began sucking on my breast. He grabbed them up and sucked like milk was coming out. This other guy rammed my pussy with his big dick and fucked me rough. He was pounding this pussy. Damn, I liked this shit. *I'm getting dick and giving head.*

After everyone had gotten their turn tasting me and fucking me, it was time for the final round. I had cum so many times by all these different-sized dicks entering me. Then tasting this sweet pussy was so amazing. Everyone came into the room for the final round. The two Chinese women poured more fruit on me and everyone got plates. The only thing that happened was they picked the fruit they wanted and walked back off stage.

When I thought it was over with, this big light-skinned chick named Big Lick'em came out strapped with a dildo. She was walking over to me, like she was ready to do some damage. I looked around at Mrs. Lee and she just stared back. They entrapped my head as this chick walked up to me. She bent down, and licked and sucked my used pussy. Finally, she stuck this all-black dildo in my pussy and began pounding me. I moaned to her every stroke. People came on stage getting more fruit off me, as they watched her fuck me. I'm enjoying all of this shit. Men and women came up squeezing my breasts, trying to get me hotter.

After about ten minutes of getting rammed hard, she stopped. She licked me some more and walked off stage.

"Are you ready to get up?" one of the women asked me.

"Yes I am," I replied.

They untied me and Dave lifted me off the table. He carried me to the back as everyone looked on. I could have walked, but he insisted on carrying me. As he carried me, fruit and cocktail juice were falling off me. This was a night I would never forget. I entered the office; Mrs. Lee came in behind us.

"Christina, are you all right?" she asked.

"Yes, I feel great," I replied, as Dave sat me on her desk.

"Okay, great. So, how did you like your first night?"

"I loved it. There were so many tongues and dicks to make me nut. I want that again," I spoke.

"Oh, really? I see you are a real freak."

"I'm freakier than you think," I spoke sarcastically.

"That's what I like to hear. Well, all the girls have left with their partner or partners; everyone else is enjoying themselves. I want you to go to the hotel and rest up. We are up to fifty thousand dollars for you."

"Fifty thousand. Damn. How much of that do I get?" I asked.

"We have to split it three ways: you, Dave and I all get a cut. It will probably go up by tomorrow night if you play your cards rights," she replied and walked out.

I looked over at Dave and he smiled, "Girl, you better get that money. I will protect you from any of them clowns. I won't let them hurt you."

"I believe you, Dave," I said, not being real sure about that. I really don't know why that came from my lips. He seemed like the type to protect me, because I was his paycheck, just as much as he was mine.

I went to the back of the club, showered, and put on my street clothes. Dave stood outside waiting for me. Stepping out, he followed me like a puppy. We walked back through the club, and they were having a fucking orgy. Bitches were getting fucked left and right. I didn't see those whores in here earlier.

"Where these chicks come from?" I asked Dave, as we walked out.

"These bitches are from downstairs. They fuck the fellows that can't afford the women like you. These are the regulars," he explained.

"Oh, really?" I said while walking out, trying to get a glimpse at the crowd.

Dave pulled up at the hotel and walked me up. As soon as I entered the room he spoke,

"I will be back tomorrow evening around six to pick you up. Don't leave the hotel until I come get you, please," he stated as he walked off. I stood in the doorway looking at him, until he

disappeared inside the elevator. Closing the door, I let out a low sigh. This was one hell of a night.

Chapter 9

I was lying in bed, feeling that soft pillow against my face, when my cell phone began to ring. That's the most annoying sound a person wants to hear when they're asleep. I turned over and looked at the hotel clock, and it read three a.m. I turned back over and just looked at the cell phone lying next to my face. I was too lazy to look at who was calling. Finally, the phone stopped ringing. I began to doze back off and this mutherfucking cell phone began ringing again. Picking it up, I saw that Peaches was calling me. Why in the hell was she calling me at this time of morning? She knows how I feel about that shit.

"Hello?" I spoke softly.

"Christy, I need you to come home," Peaches spoke while crying.

Sitting up, I asked, "What's wrong? Why are you crying?"

91

"I need to tell you something, but I don't think I should."

"Peaches, talk to me. You there?"

I could not hear her say anything. I knew she was still on the phone because she sobbed and sobbed. I really didn't know what to say to her. I'm sure that Pete had a lot to do with it. He is such an asshole at times. That nigga is always full of time. I'm beginning to believe that he is fucking other women besides me and Peaches. If he is, then I will make Peaches divorce his stupid ass. I will bring her and her kids to live with me. After she finished crying, she spoke in a different tone. Her urgency was off as she said, "Huh, huh, Pete hasn't been home since you left. I don't know where he is."

"Oh really? He hasn't called to check on you or the kids?"

"He called once to tell me not to call you, or he was going to beat me when he did get here."

"Pete threatened to beat you?"

"Yes, but please don't say anything to him," she begged.

"Why not? He knows better than to pull this type of bullshit. What the fuck is wrong with him?"

"I believe he is sleeping with this woman named Tammy. She called him the day you left, and I haven't seen him since then," Peaches explained.

"Well, I will call and talk to him."

"No, Christy, please don't tell him what I have told you! He will really beat me."

"Peaches, has Pete hit you before?" I asked, not really wanting to know the answer.

"Yes, but he hasn't done it since we met you."

I sighed and spoke, "Well, I will fix everything. You rest and take care of your kids. If it comes down to it, I will take care of you all. Do you understand me?"

"Yes, Christy, I understand."

"Okay. Get some rest and stop worrying about that jackass. You got me."

"Okay, baby," she spoke, then hung up the phone.

I hung up the cell phone on my end and thought about everything Peaches had just told me. I do remember a bitch named Tammy that Pete use to fuck with, but it can't be her. That bitch is a crackhead. Pete knows better than that shit. He knows not to bring a fucking drug addict into the picture. If he is fucking Tammy, he won't fuck me again. There is no telling what type of disease that bitch is carrying. I've been clean for years, and I'm not about to slip up. I might need to call this whore and see what's really going on. Picking up the phone to dial Pete, I put it on speakerphone. The phone rang and rang, but nobody answered it. I called four times, and this weak bitch didn't answer the phone.

After I had tossed the cell phone down on the bed, it began ringing. I grabbed it up; it was Pete calling me back.

"What's up?" he spoke.

"Where are you?" I asked.

"I'm out right now. Why?"

"I'm just checking on you. Maybe you can swing by the hotel," I stated while getting out of the bed and heading to the bathroom.

"Not tonight. I'm out with the boys right now."

"Don't sound like you are out with the boys. What the fuck are you really doing? You better not be with any of them nasty ass whores you been fucking, or you will never fuck me again."

"Christina, I'm not fucking with nasty ass whores, just you. Why are you questioning me anyway? What the fuck is up with that?" he spoke.

"Because mutherfucker, you don't have your black ass at home. Don't make me come find your stupid ass and fuck you up. I'm not playing any mutherfucking games with you. Get your fucking ass home, nigga. When I call your house phone, you better pick that bitch up," I stated as I hung up the phone in his face. *The nerve of this bitch trying to be smart, because he must have completely forgotten who the fuck I am. I will fuck up his world!* I thought in anger.

Sitting down on the toilet to take a piss, I started wondering what the hell was going on with Pete. He has never pulled this

stunt before. Shaking my head, I finished my business and went back to bed. As I lay there in bed, all I could hear was Peaches crying through the phone. This nigga was really going to make me fuck him up. He's messing with the wrong female.

Falling asleep in this comfortable bed, I began to think about Pierre. This always made me feel better when I was pissed off. All I could think about was the smell of his cologne; the touch of his hands all over my body; his soft lips against mine; and that hard body pounding against mine. Damn, I had to hurry up with this summer and go back home to my man. I had made up my mind that as soon as I touched Mississippi, I was going to marry Pierre. He had waited on me long enough.

The love I had for him was so deep, but I also felt the same way about Peaches. She had this effect on me. If Pierre and I did get married, I had to find some way to bring Peaches and her kids along. That pussy was too good for me; I don't intend to let it go. Pierre would have to understand. He can fuck Peaches too. She will do anything I tell her to do. The thought of Pierre fucking another woman never crossed my mind, but I would make the exception for Peaches. That bitch had me hooked. I could taste that pussy now. She had that pussy smelling so good every time I licked her. Then to think about her medium-sized breasts and shaved pussy, damn, it gave me chills! I smiled and fell back to sleep, dreaming of fucking Peaches.

Chapter 10

Mrs. Lee had sent Dave to pick me up late, and I didn't mind, because it was game night for me. Instead of my usual predictable self, I had to be on point. Tonight, I would find out just how much someone would pay for me and I would know just how much my cut was going to be. Smiling, I thought, *Yeah, Dave will protect me, because I am the reason he gets paid so well.* I heard a knock, and like a clock striking on time, it was Dave. Dressed in my white stilettos, matching necklace set, and pearl-white sundress that came nowhere near my knees, I looked like I was ready for someone to take me into the shade for a cooling-off.

"You look lovely as always, Christina," Dave said as he looked me over.

With arrogance, I said, "I know," as I walked passed Dave and out the door. Being the gentleman that he was, Dave opened the

door and closed it for me. *My personal body guard and steady freaking, I may not want to give this shit up, especially if Pierre is still tripping*, I thought as we drove down the highway to the club.

Arriving at the club, I was pumped, mainly after the way I got freaked out by all those mutherfuckers the other night. I was ready for a good fucking or whatever, but as soon as we walked in, NeNe came towards me. I checked her up and down, from the way her rich, huge breasts jiggled with those nice pointed nipples, to the smooth curve of her fine ass. One could only lick their lips, because if it looks that good on the outside, the pussy has to be damn good on the inside. However, I know that bitch is one of the main ones I have to let know who the bad bitch was around here, no matter how sexy her ass was.

"Christina, Mrs. Lee wants to see you," NeNe said with a cunning smile, but she just doesn't know I am going to lick her ass and spit in her pussy, just wait.

When I opened the door to the office, Mrs. Lee was sitting there in her seat, so I sat across from her, waiting to hear what she had to say.

"Christina, tonight you will not be performing."

I rose up and said, "Are you fucking kidding me? I've been waiting all week to participate."

"Christina, last night you were such a success, I had many offers for you, and to be frank, you have been the highest bid that I have ever had here."

I sat back and replied, "How much am I worth tonight?"

"Fifty thousand for the two days, because A. J. and her husband are friends of mine. I know you will please them, and that they will please you."

"When are they coming to get me?" I had to ask, because that is a lot of money for two days. But I will be worth every penny of it and more.

"They will be here around four-thirty this evening, which is in thirty minutes. They desire to take you before others have a chance to sample your good-tasting pussy. Speaking of good-tasting pussy, come here and let me taste the sample."

I walked over to her side of the desk and put my right leg up. She pulled my thong to the side and before she could get her head between my legs, I said, "No, Mrs. Lee, not right now, because I am beginning to believe that you are fond of tasting this pussy."

"I want a little taste" she said in a pleasing way, but I held my ground, even if she was the boss.

Seeing that I was not going to give in, she locked eyes with me and stuck her finger in me quickly. Then she placed it in her mouth. That foreplay was exciting to my mind. "I thought a little taste would get you ready to put out tonight."

Using a toiletry to wipe off her hand, I could only look at her, because she had no idea how much that turned me on. I placed my leg back on the floor and went back to my seat.

A knock was heard at the door, and it was the couple. The woman was nicely built and pretty to look upon. You wouldn't think that she was into freaky-ass shit like this. On the other hand, her husband was a very handsome man. I could tell that if he did this type of stuff, he only did it because of her. The way he never took his eyes off his wife, it told me that he loved her and that he wanted whatever she wanted.

The couple came over to me and the woman said, "Never mind my husband, Michael. My name is Angie Jumper, but you will call me A. J."

Before I could respond, she was already checking how perfect my body was, and I could tell it was turning her on from the way she said her name.

"How do you do, A. J.? And what a pleasure it is to be going home with you tonight."

A. J. pulled my hand up and kissed it in response. "No, the pleasure is all mine, to have you this weekend. I am eager to take you home. Shall we go?"

I walked behind her as she led the way, with her husband following behind.

Upon arriving to their home, I glanced up and saw someone peeping out the curtain, but they jumped back when they saw me looking. Their home was magnificent, and everything about it screamed rich, from the chandlers to the expensive paintings hanging on the wall. My mind was blown away, because they had an elevator that went up three stories and down to the basement.

While standing in their hallway looking like a tourist, a young voice came from behind me saying, "You like the view?"

It was a young girl. She appeared to be no more than my age, if not a year younger.

"Yes, thank you. The home is quite elegant and fashionably put together," I said, checking out the female in front of me. She was very nicely shaped. She didn't have on a bra, and I loved her very perky breasts. Her stomach was flat with a belly ring. The blue jean shorts were cutting her in all the right places, and now I wanted to fuck this bitch and not the old bitch. But if I play right, I can have my cake and eat it too.

She walked up closer to me and said, "I like your style; hopefully you will play with me before you leave."

"Tomorrow night, be my supper and don't be late," I said with a hungry smile. If I can play with her I will, for sure. From the back of me, she saw the older lady come up

The girl said, "Nice meeting you," then she walked off.

"I see you have met my foster daughter, Erica," A. J. said.

Smiling, I replied, "Yes, we were chatting about how beautiful your home is."

"Good. I was an only child. Therefore, I am selfish, and if she wants a toy, she better buy her own. I get angry when I am forced to share." Then she walked off. I know now I have to play the good girl because of the tone she used. I better perform my ass off every time she calls on me. To my surprise, she did not want me yet, and that's good because that means I have only one day left before I leave. This money is easy to make, and if she chooses to waste it, so be it. I took a shower and went to bed.

It's Saturday morning; and I am beginning to wonder when the fun will begin. I'm horny and in heat. I refuse to please myself with all this pussy in this house, I'll be damned, I thought as I heard the knock at the door. "Come in," I said in a happy tone.

I was feeling a little disappointed because it was the maid; however, I made up my mind to try her, since the house was quiet and the real time hadn't begun.

"You want your pussy ate? I don't have to play in it, just use my tongue to please you," I said.

"I don't know, the Misses gets angry if her toy is fooling around with the hired help," she said, as she started straightening things up.

"Who is going to tell? I'm sure not," I said, trying to get her to go along.

"I don't know, ma'am," she said as she looked at me.

"You mean to tell me that getting your pussy ate doesn't sound good?" I said, as she looked my way.

"I, I, I am not sure about this," the maid said nervously, as she contemplated taking me up on my offer.

Uncovering my body and scooting down in the bed, I replied, "Well, if fun is what you are waiting for, come on in!"

To my amazement, she said in a dry voice, "I am going to have to decline."

I couldn't believe my ears, and truthfully, I didn't give a fuck, and that's why I walked right up to her and lifted up the short maid dress. Right there on the floor, I lay down and pulled her down on top of my face. She was a little perfumed up with a little sweat between her legs, but that scent enticed me more because it was risky and my adrenaline was pumping. Placing her pussy on my mouth, I began to eat. Using my tongue to enter her, I massaged her inside as far as I could go.

After a few minutes of pulling and twisting on her pussy, she came and I dismissed her. But the joke was on me. She declined the dismissal and led me in the direction of the bed. I had already cum, so she had served her purpose to me, but that didn't stop her. She twisted my clit in a position that my toes wiggled, like they were waving hello. The more she did that, the more I hit her ass and licked her ass. She wasn't stopping, and that was what I liked -

she was a freak, and she was mutherfucking good. I tried to hang in with her, but for the first time, someone outdid me.

But she was the hired help, and in my eyes she didn't count, so I flipped her around. I licked her ass, and moved my head back and forth on her pussy. She began to pump my face out of control, and that shit excited me. The hired maid made me rock her body trying to get all she had to give, and she let go of my clit and put all her energy in moving on my face. *Yeah, I'm in control again*, I thought. As her body released the wet stuff, she sat flat on my face, but I made her move by not stopping the taste-testing. I was in my own groove and taking the maid on a cleaning spree, when a knock was heard at the door. The maid eased up and pretended to do work, while I acted like I just woke up. I said, "Come in."

It was A. J. She looked at me strangely and then at the maid and said, "What took you so long to answer?"

"I was asleep. What's up?" I said, as if I really just woke up, but the truth was I was tired now, that bitch in the black-and-white dress had worn me the fuck out, and I needed to sleep.

"I was checking to see if you wanted to hang out for a few minutes today?" A. J. said.

"Give me a few minutes to get up and I'll be downstairs," I said.

She made it to the door and turned to the maid and said, "You may get the fuck out so she can get up."

A.J. did not move until the maid moved. The maid dropped her head and left. Damn that bitch. I wasn't finished with the maid. I hit the bed with my fist a few times, because I was just getting started, even if I was tired. Sighing, I got up and got dressed, because money is time and I was on her time.

As I walked downstairs, I tapped the maid on the ass and said, "I want some more of that hot sweaty ass before I leave."

"Sorry, I'm about to get off and you can't get away from here," she said.

I looked disappointed, and then I heard Erica and her mom talking. Walking carefully, I stopped short of the door and Erica said, "Why won't you fuck me? Is it because of my dad? It can be like old times, baby."

"No! Bitch, you talk too much. You'll tell him that I had you before I had him, and you are not going to ruin the shit I have going," A. J. said.

"He always leaves when you bring over toys, and right now, he would never have to know of me eating your beautiful pussy," Erica said as she touched her mom between the legs.

"If you can stay away from this toy, I'll let you have me all to yourself when she leaves," A. J. said.

"And use toys too?" Erica asked.

"And use toys too," A. J. said

To them I am a game; I will show those conniving bitches, I thought as I said loudly to break up their conversation, "Hello, A. J.? Where are you?"

"I'm here, come on in," A. J. said.

When I walked in, I said, "Am I interrupting something?"

Brushing off Erica, A. J. said, "Nothing as important as you. Come. Breakfast is ready."

I walked by Erica and she touched my hand. That let me know that she was down and ready, whenever I was.

We ate breakfast in silence. Once we were finished, A. J. said, "I'm sorry, but I can't show you around. I will call you when I am ready for you. Erica is busy, so she can't show you either."

"I am?" Erica said in a surprised manner.

"Yes, you are, you have to go uptown and pick out a few things while I am gone. The maid is leaving, so you'll be here alone. Will you be all right?"

"That is fine; I can use the extra sleep," I said.

Seeing everyone leave, I felt alone, but it felt nice to rest because I know a show is going on tonight. Deciding to go in their sweat box, I stripped off and decided to enjoy the heat. When I opened the door naked, I was stunned to see Michael.

He said as he dropped his head, "I thought you left with the others."

"I thought you were gone as well," I replied, covering up.

"I do leave, but I double back while everyone is away for peace of mind," he said sadly.

As I walked in, I grabbed a towel off the rack and sat a few feet from him and asked, "Why do you need peace of mind?" I just had to know.

"My daughter and wife have been fucking. At least, they used to, and they think I don't know," he said candidly.

"Wow. How do you feel about that?" I said, because he seemed like a great guy.

"Well, I was lonely with an adopted daughter. I needed a companion and a mother for her, not a damn lover for her," he said as he sounded angry.

"They have their secret, let me be yours," I said.

I walked to him. I got on my knees and took his long dick into my mouth. The heat and the sweat didn't bother me, because I had the fever for a man.

He moaned and said, "I shouldn't do this, I love my wife."

I tasted his salty dick a little more and said, "You may love her but right now, let me love you with no strings attached."

He pushed my head on his dick a little more and moaned. I began to lick up and down his hearty shaft, even sucking at the vein.

"Damn, a woman has never tasted this before," he said.

I licked tenderly around his dick and sucked on the tip. His dick wasn't too long, so sucking all of him was not a problem. Each time I took my mouth off him, he said, "Please don't stop, it's good, damn good."

I licked more and more to make him lose his breath. I put his nut sack in my mouth, and he screamed out. If someone was near, they would have heard him for sure, but I continued since it was his money those bitches were throwing around. He deserved a treat. My tongue began to slither up and down his dick, and from time to time, I would use my hand to give him a personal hand job.

"Please put your hot mouth back on me, so I can fill you with the first one," he begged.

Following orders like a good girl, I did. "When you nut, look at me," I instructed.

Michael was taking my head and holding it on his dick as I sucked my way out. "Baby, I'm about to…"

He couldn't finish his sentence because his eyes were glued on my eyes, as I drank from his stick. When I pulled up, his sperm was dripping from my mouth. I was trying to create a scene so he could remember who freaked him out. He was enjoying the show; therefore, I took my hand and scooped the rest of him up in my mouth. He shuddered.

"May I enter you?" he asked, with his dick still ready.

I lay back on the floor with my legs on the benches, so he could fall between my legs and into this hot pussy.

"May I touch it?" he asked, like a little boy who was told not to touch something he desperately wanted to.

"I'm yours for now, touch what the hell you want. Better yet, stop asking and take it," I said.

He took his big hand and inserted all his fingers inside me. I wanted to get angry because I have never let anyone do that, but because he was an older man with that cheddar, I closed my mouth. After playing in my pussy for a few minutes, I asked, "Are you going to fuck me or what?"

He put his fingers in my mouth, and I sucked them. Michael jerked his hand away and jumped on top of me.

At first he didn't know what to do, but he arched his back and guided his shaft into my warm water. A few moments later, and we were in rhythm. *This bastard is actually good*, I thought as he rode me like a gentleman. I closed my eyes and pretended that he was Pierre. That thought caused me to lock my legs around him and pull him deeper.

He kept moaning and saying, "This is good, damn, this is good. Be my toy, please be my toy."

To keep him excited and using my psychology, I said, "It's yours, it's yours, and I'll be your toy. Keep going, papi, that's it,

that's it." Then I pretended to yell a little, "Oh yeah, I can't take that, this dick is good, this dick is good!"

Like a charm, he nutted and kept pumping his ass, as if he was leaving a baby off in it. Luckily, I am protected by Mirena. If I wasn't, I'm sure I would be fucked right now. When he sat up, I scrambled between his legs and licked all of the flavor off his soft shaft.

"Please stop, I can't take anymore. You're trying to give an old man a heart attack," he said with a smile.

"No. I'm just pleasing someone that truly deserves it and it was good," I told him to get in his head, and it worked.

"Give me your account number, I'm going to leave you a surprise. Mrs. Lee and A. J. will not know it. It's straight cash and you don't have to share."

"You're going to give me a surprise? Really? Why?" I said.

"You have pleased me like no other. My wife has never done that to me. In fact, this is the first time I have ever done anything like this, and I have never paid for a woman...not for myself, anyway. Your discretion is needed. I want you to be the only woman I sleep with. You think you can do that?" he asked, almost shyly.

"What about the love you have for your wife?"

"I do love my wife, but we haven't had sex together in years. I am willing to pay you top dollar for a little bit every now and then."

I looked at him in his begging formation and replied, "No one will know of the fun we did here, but anytime you need a fixer-upper, come get me. By the way, learn how to eat pussy. I love that shit," I said as I left him alone.

With all this fucking shit going on, I thought, *Can a bitch get some sleep?* I laughed as my conscience said, *You are here to work, you can sleep later.* I went back to my room, showered, and went to sleep.

When I woke up, I called the twenty-four hour banking number, and I had to call it again because when it said, "Fifty thousand", I wanted to jump for joy. I had fifty grand that was not touched by Mrs. Lee, and to make sure, I opened up another bank account and transferred all my money into it, just in case the old man had any funny ideas. "I need to freak him more often," I thought, and I couldn't shake the grin off my face.

That night at supper when I arrived, Erica was there sitting down. She told me that A.J. would be late and that her father would probably be gone until Monday.

I looked around and asked the young vixen, "Do you feel like playing open, come get it with me?"

"I have never heard of that game before."

"All you have to do is open your legs where you are, while I come get it."

Her facial expression showed her surprise, but she scooted to the edge of the chair and placed her legs over each arm of the chair. Acting cocky, Erica gave me that I'm-down-for-whatever look, and that was enough for me.

Lifting up the table cloth, I proceeded to get on my legs and left elbow, because in my right hand was the light on my cell phone. Making her wait, I took my time, for she did not need to know when she was being captured by my tongue. Coming closer to her, I used my fingers to mark my territory, and she jumped. Just as I thought, she wore a shirt dress with no panties, perfect, for I could smell the cucumber-melon scent, and it got me heated. But the only problem was, she was hairy. *It's been a long time since I had a hairy pussy*, I thought as I touched her twat with the back of my left hand, feeling the hair brush against my skin.

I looked closely at the fruit that was severely hidden in the mist of vines, but I continued because I desired to taste the young, inexperienced lady. Turning to my cell phone, I placed it on silent and used the light to view her pink but fluffy pussy. Putting my cell phone between her legs, I placed my index fingers and thumbs together to pull back the hair, and before my eyes was a perfectly-shaped pussy. It looked like it had never had anything in it, and that thought turned me on. As I placed my lips on her and French-

kissed it, she moaned. With her bottom exposed to me in a great position, I dove in and tasted the clit. The girl got wet, and I began to play with her wetness with my tongue. She started moaning and moving, but I pinched her and I said, "Shut the fuck up. Do you want to get caught?"

She replied in a rasping voice, "I don't want you to stop. I promise I will be quieter."

After hearing her speak, my tongue went deeper into her pussy, and it tasted good. Using the light off my cell, I looked closer at her wet pussy, it was budding and ready to explode. But I needed to slow her down, so I used my two fingers and played in her pussy. She started moving a little, but I told her to be still and she did. Like a natural, she raised her ass up and shot cum everywhere. I told her to be quiet and hold on. When I began tasting her more, I heard, A.J. say, "Have you seen my new toy, bitch?"

Not able to speak clearly, Erica said with an attitude, "Gee golly, Mommy, I haven't seen your new toy, but it's a toy that I wouldn't mind playing with."

Walking closer, A. J. said, "Bitch, do not play. I paid good-ass money to have her, but since you want to play, you pay. Remember this morning? I get the first taste, the first sample of that caramel-ass bitch, then you pay to play. But if you get it before me, there will be hell to pay."

Trying to keep a straight face was hard because Erica moaned, then A. J. said, "Why the hell are you moaning and no one is here?"

"I thought about how much fun it's going to be to play with her, that's all," Erica said.

Unsure if she believed her foster daughter or not, she replied, "I'm watching your no-good stinking ass." She walked off and slammed the door.

Not stopping my groove, I sucked harder because I know that these two bitches are playing a game with me. But I will play dumb and turn them against each other, because that's what freaks like me do, fuck 'em and leave 'em. In a flash, Erica started grinding on my face, and all that nut belonged to me. I wasn't sure I wanted to leave her alone, because overall, she tasted sweet and I can eat all day when the pussy is sweet and young. Backing away from the table, I stood. "What did A. J. want?" I asked.

"She was looking for you. I want to nut some more. When can you make me do it?" Erica said.

"If you play fair, probably tonight after I see your mom," I told her, because I wanted to stick something in that pussy, I didn't care if it was just my face. I used the napkin to wipe my face, and now I was ready to get my freak on.

I walked up the stairs and saw A. J. standing in the mirror naked. She was bending over and touching her toes. Her spread

was awesome, and for her to be an older lady, she still looked good, especially from that angle. I opened the door and stood there with a smile. She turned towards me and I closed the door as I walked in. Carefully observing, I saw a carousel horse, and instantly I knew how I was going to play these bitches.

"I heard you been looking for me," I said, with her pussy on my mind.

She walked over to the closet and pulled out some toys, and I got excited because this was the shit I had been looking for. I should have known this old freak had the shit. She lay on the bed on rose petals, and damn, she looked good enough to eat.

"Where is your husband?" I demanded to know, as I walked over to examine the toys.

A. J. smiled as she saw me touching the toys and replied, "To begin with, I have paid an extra ten thousand for your ass to Mrs. Lee, because I see I have a little competition and I don't like losing. As for my husband, he's out on business, and I'm in the mood for some kinky shit."

Taking my hand, I touched the entire length of her body while she lay on the bed with her eyes closed. When I made it to her nipples, I had to sneak a little taste, and I tasted apples. Not able to stop, I sucked more. I decided to make love to her, because she's an old hen that believes that a young woman like me can't make her run in the bed. Getting in the bed next to her, I started kissing

her as I fingered her. She was very wet, and I figured I would take care of her first, before I added the surprise twist. I started at the breasts, for they were juicy and implants. That didn't matter though; they were nicely-shaped and a handful. I made my way below the navel and patted it. She jumped; that told me she was ready. Easing lower on her body, I played with her pussy and teased her, not really wanting to enter her, but controlling her. She doesn't run shit here but her mouth, and tonight I'm going to stop that too.

"Come on, taste it," she said. "Come on, taste it, taste it," she begged more.

I gave her a little taste just to settle her down, and then I got aroused and began tasting her with love. She would move her body slowly and I would ride her slowly with my tongue.

"Why don't you take me fast?" she begged.

"You are always in a rush, and tonight I run things," I told her.

She saw her sweetness around my mouth and nose, and then she saw when I reached for the strap-on and tied it up on me. Being experienced, she put her legs on my shoulder and I entered her easily, then I started pumping her like a man.

"Take this dick," I would tell her as she moaned with pleasure.

"Who fucking you like you want, huh? Who fucking you like you want?" I told her.

"You are, my toy, you are!" she screamed.

★ ★ ★ ★ 115

Psychologically, if you can get into someone's mind when you make them feel good, you can whip any mutherfucker you wish, and sadly enough, I know this.

"That's right," I would tell her when my rhythm settled, as I pushed all eleven inches inside her. When I felt that she was about to bust, I would stop and say, "You enjoying this dick?"

She was dazed and couldn't respond as she wanted. She only said, "More, enter me more."

I would then go slower, and when she nutted, I got off her and licked her. Tasting fresh juice as it runs out the warm faucet is good, and sucking her drove her wild.

"Get on the edge of the bed and bring that pussy to me," I told her in haste.

She got on all fours and I stood up behind her. First I licked her ass and used my fingers to open her up, and then I easily entered that soft ass of hers. She broke down to her elbows.

"No, you stupid bitch, get up and take this dick." I said to her.

"No one has ever been in there," she said with a tremble.

"I promise you will enjoy it," I said, knowing all along I tend to get rough.

She got back up; I went slow and made her ass drop in my lap. I would hold her sides and bang that asshole, rocking side to side as if I was stepping to a dance. It became good to her because her moans increased, and she nutted and fell on her face.

"No one has ever fucked me like that," A. J. said and then growled at me. It took everything in me to hold back my laugh.

"Are you willing to trust me; that what goes on in here stays in here?"

"Anything for you," she said.

That was all I needed to hear. I opened the door and Erica came in.

"What the fuck is this bitch doing in here?" A. J. screamed in anger.

"Shut the fuck up, A. J. I'm running this damn show and you will participate. I know that y'all done fucked, and tonight we all going to fuck," I said.

Erica pulled off her clothes; I walked to the carousel and strapped the dick on its back. "Who's going to ride it first?" I asked the two.

Erica replied, "I will."

When she got on the strap on and we watched her grind for a few minutes, I couldn't help it. I got between A. J's legs and started tasting her to the rhythm of Erica's moans. A. J. was losing her mind, as she watched Erica's breasts jump. When Erica nutted, she got up and I sucked the firm dick she was riding, and it tasted ever so sweet. Then A. J. put on the strap on and took me from the back, while I ate Erica. Somehow, I loved tasting Erica. Her pussy was hairy, but underneath the hair was a prize. I came and A. J.

sucked romantically on my clit and lips. She can't whip a bitch like me; I'm not weak, but it was damn close though. When A. J. licked my pussy up, I had to have Erica.

"Oh hell no, you can't fuck Erica, that's my personal pussy," A.J. said.

"Well, I want to dive my face and this huge dick in the pussy, and freak her out," I said, just to test A. J.

"Didn't I fucking say no? You can fuck me, but you can't fuck her," A. J. said again.

"Okay. I won't fuck her. Let me watch you fuck her," I said, challenging A.J.

A.J. donned the strap-on, climbed on top of Erica, and fucked her hard. I felt sorry for her, but assumed she was punishing her for wanting to fuck someone other than her. As I watched them act like tigers, I sat back and waited to see who went to sleep first. As luck would have it, A. J. passed out first. While she was asleep, Erica got on the floor. I strapped up, and fucked her out. The way she held my body and sucked my breasts as I rode her made me feel too damn good. I didn't want to stop banging her, even when she nutted and fell asleep, I ate her pussy. She was too weak to fight me off, so I left her alone and went back to the bed and started on A. J. At the first flick of my tongue, she woke up and rolled her pussy on my face. I was trying to put my entire face in

her small hole just to make her feel special. The deeper my tongue went, the harder she rolled. I got up and told her to ride.

She mounted me like a pro. If I were a real man, I would have enjoyed it more. Anyway, all I had to do was lay there and let her hurt herself. It didn't take long, because just like a ship coming in, she leaned closer to me like she was a jockey taking the dick, bouncing her ass on the long, hard, strap-on dick.

"You damn bitch, you damn toy, fuck you, fuck you." A. J. said, then she rolled off me and went back to sleep.

Watching the two of them sleep, I got up and had to get a drink, because I was feeling worn out. The maid was gone and Michael was gone; there was no need to cover up. I made it to the kitchen and Michael was there. "Why are you home early?" I asked.

"I knew you had the two asleep, and I wanted to try something with you," he said.

I wasn't tired and could use some more of his dick, so I followed him up stairs. When we made it to the top stair, he stopped.

"Sit your butt here, I want to eat your pussy," he said, as if it took a lot of courage.

When I sat with my legs wide open, he smiled and said, "You look beautiful, and I have never done this before."

"Pretend it is your favorite food and you haven't had it in a long time," I told him.

He laid his head between my legs and started biting me. "What the fuck you trying to do?" I yelled at him.

He looked ashamed and sad, so I said, "Be gentle with me, please, I know you can."

This time he took his time and tasted me perfectly. He was a gentleman. When I busted that nut, it took everything out of me, but he kept on going, trying to blow my mind. After I had a big orgasm, I laid there and he said, "Stay with me…"

"I can't, but I promise I will come back when you call." He didn't even let me finish my sentence; he just walked away with his head down. Instead of going to sleep, I called Dave to pick me up. My job here was done.

Chapter 11

Damn, that was a long-ass weekend with A.J and Michael. How good it felt to fuck them both, but I couldn't wait until I got Peaches and Pete in bed together. It would be so much better because I have feelings for them. Come to think about it, today is Wednesday, and I haven't talked to Peaches in a couple of days. Pete must have taken his ass home and did what the fuck I told him to do. Looking around and becoming disgusted, I thought, *I'm still looking at these damn hotel walls; I'm ready to take my ass home. Mrs. Lee just will have to understand. She has me hidden, so I won't fuck anyone outside of the club. This bitch must be crazy!*

I was packing my shit, ready to get the fuck out of there, when Mrs. Lee called. The cell phone was ringing and I really didn't want to answer that mutherfucker, but against my better judgment, I did.

"Hello," I spoke with an attitude.

"Did you enjoy your weekend?" Mrs. Lee asked.

"Yes, but today is Wednesday. Why didn't you call to check on me Monday?" I demanded an answer from Mrs. Lee.

"Because when Dave dropped you off, he reported to me that you were safe. Why the fuck should I call you? I'm running this mutherfucker. I'm the HBIC, not you. Don't ever question me about anything I do or don't do for you. Do we have an understanding?" she stated.

"Yes, I do understand, but you still should have called me."

"Well, maybe I should have. Anyway, I called you to let you know to get ready for tonight. I have a client by the name of Dawn Wallace who has reserved you for tonight," she spoke.

"I have to fuck her by myself? No man is going to be involved?" I replied.

"No, Christina, you won't have a hard dick tonight to fuck. Damien and I will take care of that when you come back."

"Damn, how long am I going to be with her?" I asked.

"She only wants you for tonight. Don't worry about all that. Just shave your pussy, and don't forget to soak in the honey and milk."

"Cool," I stated as I hung up the phone.

Tossing the cell phone on the bed, I began to unpack my bags. My pussy began beating as I thought about how I was going to

dominate this female. I wanted to ram my purple dildo all in her ass or perhaps lick her clit while running my index finger in her ass. A smile came over my face when suddenly my cell phone began to ring. The song *Love Faces* by Trey Songz sounded throughout the hotel room. That was Pierre's ring tone. Jumping down on the bed; I answered the phone with my sexy voice. "Hi baby."

"What's up, Ma? What you doing?"

"Sitting here on the bed thinking about you fucking me, of course."

"Really? That means your pussy is hot and I need to come fuck you," he spoke.

"Yes, big daddy, come fuck me."

"Don't tempt me; you know I miss that sweet-ass pussy."

"Is that all you miss, nigga?" I asked jokingly.

"Hell no, I want you to come home. Your parents and I have all the money you need; you don't need to work for nobody," he explained.

"I know, Pierre, but I want my own money. Your money is your money and my parent's money is their money. Why won't you people let me grow up? I'm trying to take care of me, without help."

"We are; we just love your sexy ass. Damn, baby I'm missing you so fucking much. I really need to take some time out to come

up there. I want to know what you doing anyway. Knowing you, you are doing some wild shit. I better not come up there and you fucking another nigga."

"Boy, don't play. You are the only nigga I'm fucking and sucking," I lied.

"I better be, because you know I will come up there and act a damn donkey on who the fuck ever," he spoke with a thug mentality.

"Stop it. I'm not fucking anyone," I said, but was glad he could not see the look on my face.

"Well, I'm just saying. I have to go baby, I just wanted to check in with your sexy ass."

"Okay baby. I love you so much."

"I love you too," Pierre replied.

We hung up the phone and I laid out on the bed. I was staring at the ceiling, thinking about how I had just lied to Pierre. I have never lied to him before, and here I was spitting game. He knew something was up. I just hope he really didn't get a ticket and come on. He would always do some crazy shit, but yet he talked about me doing crazy things. Pierre had a valid point. Why was I working? It wasn't about the money. It was about the different men and women I could fuck. I'm from the small town of Forest, and we don't have anything like this around town. I'd always wanted to

experience different sexual acts, and now I had the chance to do it all. There was no limit to what I could do in Delicious Divas.

Getting up off the bed and shutting down my fantasy of different men and women fucking me, I ran the tub with lukewarm water, and poured in the honey and milk with a little bubble bath. After lighting strawberry-scented candles in the small bathroom, I began taking off my clothes piece by piece, admiring my body. My bra fell to the floor as my breasts stood out with hard nipples. Grabbing both of them, I squeezed and squeezed myself, pulling on my nipples to make them stand out further. Chills ran down my spine as I continued to pull off my pants and thongs. Looking down at my pussy, I grabbed the Nair and lathered myself up. After that, I walked back to the bed and grabbed my small radio. I plugged it within the bathroom and let the soft melody take me away. "Emergency" by Tank sang out. I couldn't turn it up too loud, because I didn't want the manager or anyone knocking on my door, and make me have to go the fuck off.

Carefully wiping the Nair away from my pussy, I watched myself in the big mirror. It really turned me on to look at my own body. After I cleaned up the Nair, I jumped in the tub to relax. I lowered my body down. The water rushed between my legs, giving me more chills, and then it hit my breasts as if caressing one's mouth over them. Sitting down and slowly falling backwards, I

began to relax. Taking the cloth, I ran the small warm towel up and down my body. I caressed each and every part of my body.

After scrubbing for about ten minutes, I decided to close my eyes and pretend I was in a far away country like Nigeria, fucking their men. I licked my lips just thinking about it. Beginning to rub my pussy under the water, I thought about the fact that a strange woman would love me tonight. It would be impossible for me to cum right now, because I wanted her so bad. It excited me because I didn't know what she looked like. Taking my hands away, I just relaxed for about an hour.

As I got out of the tub, there was a soft knock at my door. I turned off the radio and walked over to the door, peeping out the peep hole. It was Dave. A smile came over my face, and I opened the door.

"Hi Dave, why are you here?" I asked.

"Mrs. Lee told me to come down and scoop you up."

"Where am I going this early?"

"She wanted me to bring you down to the club," he stated as his eyes rolled up and down my body, staring like a dog in heat.

"Okay. Give me a few minutes to get dressed," I replied.

"I will be waiting in the car for your sexy ass," he remarked.

"Sweet," I stated, while closing the door on him. Dave was standing there as if I was going to invite him in. I wasn't going to

fuck him. I needed him to be levelheaded. This sweet pussy would have him crazy for sure.

Thirty minutes went by, and I was headed out the door. I grabbed my purse and an overnight bag. There is no telling what there is in store for me tonight.

"It's about time you brought your ass out of there," Dave spoke sarcastically.

"You know I have to be looking and smelling my best. Don't want to have a bad pussy day and neither one of us gets paid," I spoke.

"I guess you are right, but I don't see you having a fucked-up-smelling pussy."

"No. I keep her cleaned up and well groomed."

We both laughed and headed to the club. I was actually looking out into the city. As Dave drove on, I thought about Paris. I hadn't heard from that bitch. What the hell was really going on? "Have you seen Paris?" I asked Dave.

"Yeah. She has been very busy. You know she is trying to compare herself to you with Mrs. Lee. You need to watch out for her. I don't think she is a true friend. Besides, I hear her girlfriend Peach broke it off with her, but Paris can't let her go." He spoke as if he knew something that I didn't know, but needed to know.

"Why would you say all of that?"

"I'm back in the cut, but I listen. Just trust me, boo; she is not your friend. That bitch has something against you. She knows that you are #1 right now, and that's all Mrs. Lee cares about right now."

"Is that right?" I asked in surprise.

"Yes. You are the bomb, and she has taken to you so quickly. Mrs. Lee never comes to visit anyone. And she damn sure doesn't taste anyone's pussy. You are special. Believe that. Just watch that bitch Paris, I'm telling you."

I looked at him, and he was dead serious. I didn't know much about Dave, but I felt deep down that this nigga wasn't lying. I just hoped shit didn't go sour with me and Paris. She has been my best friend for almost four years now. I laid my head back on the headrest and just closed my eyes.

Chapter 12

When I finally walked into the club, that mutherfucker was jumping. *Plenty Money* by Plies was sounding out through the speakers. Feeling that shit beat through my chest, I walked in with my ass cheeks moving up and down like I was a million dollar bitch, and I knew my walk was so deadly. I looked and felt like a model; my hips swayed back and forth. I put on my million dollar smile and walked to Mrs. Lee's office like I was the shit. As I looked out at the stage, three of the girls watched me. They had this sour-ass look on their faces. I didn't give a fuck, because I was the shit. Nobody could tell me different.

"I see you are here, baby," Mrs. Lee spoke.

"Yes, ma'am."

"You did what I tell you to do?"

"Yes, I did. Would you like to smell me?" I spoke as I walked over to her.

I leaned down, putting my breasts in her face. She took her face and stuck it between my two girls. She swayed her head back and forward while sniffing.

"Yes, you are very clean," she stated.

"See, I'm a good girl. I can follow orders," I spoke.

"That's good to know," she stated with this silly smirk on her face.

"What do I do now, since I'm not performing on stage tonight?"

"Well, we have a small show we want to do tonight."

"Where and with whom?" I asked.

"Well, you will go to the underground stage and rise up into the club. Ms. Dawn Wallace, who has paid for you tonight, will come up and join you. She will eat you right there. We have this guy that we picked out to come up and fuck you right there as well. Then you will go home with Dawn," she explained.

"I will be fucking them in front of the whole club?" I said with a crazy look on my face.

"Hell yeah. Will that be a problem?" she stated, as she stood up out of her chair to assert her authority.

"I don't want to fuck in front of all those people," I said like a three-year-old pouting.

Mrs. Lee walked over to me and stood in my face. She was staring at me as I stared back at her. Then she stated, "You will do whatever the fuck I tell you to do. And you will fuck in front of the clients. We can make plenty more money if you fuck out there…TONIGHT!" she yelled.

"Why me? Why not get them other bitches to do it?"

"Because they are old news. You are what I want, and although I don't like to share my personal goods, that's what you are here for."

"Well, find another bitch," I stated, as I began to walk out.

Dave blocked the door and Mrs. Lee rushed over to me, slamming me against the wall. She turned me around so fast and spoke, "Bitch, don't make me beat the shit out of you before you go on. Now, you will do whatever I fucking tell you. You are fucking tonight. Do we have a problem?" she snapped while putting her hand around my throat squeezing.

"No, ma'am," I struggled to say, due to the lack of airflow.

"Good. Now get your ass ready. You will go in my bathroom to get dressed. I don't want them other bitches influencing you about anything," she said, while pointing towards the bathroom.

I put my head down and headed to the bathroom. I wanted to turn around and bust that bitch upside the head. If she ever grabbed me like that again, I would show her what a Mississippi ass-

whipping looked like. Theses bitches in Denver were fucking crazy, but they got the right bitch to toy with.

Dressing in this whole body black cat suit with a mask, I looked like a real slut. Looking in the mirror at myself; I turned around and bounced my ass up and down. Had to make sure the suit wasn't too tight. My ass looked so big and fluffy.

I looked down between my legs, and the crouch was missing. It exposed my shaved pussy. My breasts were popping out like blueberry muffins. I turned around to all angles to make sure I was looking good.

Walking out into the office, Dave grabbed me by the arm, leading me to the underground stage. Mr. and Mrs. Lee looked closely as I strutted out.

"Are you ready?" Dave spoke as he closed the office door.

"Yes, I am. I have no choice."

"Are you all right?" he asked, as if he was concerned.

"Yes, I'm good."

"I will be near, just in case things get out of hand. Just give me that eye–to-eye contact and I will stop the show," he spoke.

"Thanks, Dave. You are so sweet," I replied back, as I prepared for the stage.

I got on the stage and propped myself up. I had to wait until eight o' clock came around. It seemed like it was taking forever. My heart was pounding like no tomorrow. I was beginning to

sweat and shit. These niggas needed to hurry up. I was excited to see the crowd and what was in store for me.

"Hey. Are you okay?" this familiar voice called out.

I looked around to see Paris standing there, looking like a school girl in green and white stripes. Her hair was in two pig tails like Pippi Longstocking. "Why do you care?" I snapped back.

"Because I'm your best friend, bitch," she spoke.

"Bitch, you disappeared on me. You haven't called me or texted me. Your friend Peaches has you that wrapped up that you forget about me? You have been a totally different bitch since we came back to Denver," I stated.

"I apologize, and my friend Peaches wants to tell her girl about us, but I am totally against it. As for here, Christina, this is my job, and you will only be here for a month or two. I will always be here, and Mrs. Lee is falling head–over-heels about you."

"That's not my fucking problem. You are supposed to be my friend, not my enemy."

"I'm not your enemy. Those bitches in the club are your enemies. I do have your back, Christina. Those bitches are jealous, and they will do anything to get rid of you. I promise that won't happen. You just watch your back," she stated as she walked back out the door with an attitude.

My mind started wandering. I noticed that since I have been here, none of them has anything to say to me. It really didn't

bother me, because not one of these bitches was paying my way for anything, and I didn't socialize well with other grown bitches, so fuck those whores.

More thoughts took over but flashed away when the stage began moving upwards. I got myself together and posted up. The music became so loud. The speakers were jumping off the wall with mad bass. As the stage opened to the club, so many people gathered around staring at me. Three big sixty-four-inch Vizio plasma televisions glowed amongst the wall. "Player of the Month" flashed on each screen with different photos of me. I wondered how the hell they got those pictures. Then I thought about Paris; she had all types of pictures of me. The lights became very dim where I couldn't look out into the crowd, as the glow from the televisions sparked.

Suddenly, the stage began turning around in circles. It appeared on the televisions. I smiled and continued to look like a million-dollar bitch. As the stage turned around, there was this big black rough-looking female standing there at the edge of the stage. Giving her a beauty pageant wave, I smiled, showing all my teeth. In the back of my mind, I was hoping this wasn't Dawn Wallace. She looked more like King Kong, with nappy-ass hair.

The stage stopped and she rushed over to me. She bent down between my legs and gently opened them. She went down and began blowing in my pussy. Pretending she was someone else or I

was somewhere else, I closed my eyes and leaned my head backwards, as Dawn ran her nose up my pussy then lightly touched it with her tongue. It felt so good compared to the purple bearskin rug lying underneath me. Just by her doing this, I could sense that she was experienced in sexual pleasure. The men and women from the crowd began cheering and yelling out. As she sucked my pussy harder, I had to open my eyes and stare at her tasting my honey.

I looked around the club. We were displayed on the televisions to everyone. I had to put on a show. Therefore, I arched my back some, just enough to throw it to her a little, then popped it back just enough to tease her. She rose up, looked at me with an "I got you bitch" look, then she began sticking her fingers in my pussy while licking my clit. A sensational rush was coming over me, and I knew that the first nut was coming soon. I didn't understand how a woman as hard up as I am, would nut this early in the game. Not to let on, I lay back down as she stuck one finger in, then two fingers. I was hoping she didn't go with three, because I would have to slap that bitch. My pussy has been fucked many times, but not that many to be open like that. She was truly gifted in the art of pleasure, because I had to hold in my screams as she began moving those fingers in and out with perfection. I tightened my ass cheeks, because the ugly bitch made me cum right there on stage. I glanced down at her and she knew she had completed her mission, because

she smiled at me, took out her fingers, and placed them in her mouth.

Suddenly, this guy jumped on stage. I was looking at him as Dawn moved out of the way. He took me by the hand and lifted me up. He motioned me to get on my knees. I got down as Dawn fondled my breasts. Looking back, I saw him with his pants pulled down. He put on a condom and entered me roughly. I jumped and yelled out. He was fucking me like a rabbit. Dawn walked offstage as Nene stepped on stage with her white-and-black nurse uniform on. She walked over to me, leaned down, and began tongue-kissing me as this guy fucked me hard.

As she kissed me, she whispered in my ear, "Here is a little something to help you through the night." She continued to kiss me and slid a pill in my mouth. I swallowed and she got up. This guy pushed me over and jumped down on top of me. He rushed back in me hard and began just straight fucking me like a wild animal. Nene stepped over me and bent down, placing her pretty-ass pink pussy in my face. The pussy was looking like a budding flower in the spring and I was the bee. With her heels on, the wide open pussy was in position for me to taste and play with it, leaving her clit ready to be sucked. I began licking and sucking on her clit, as this wild man had his way with me. As I lay there, this pill was causing me to feel a little dizzy, but that was a damn good feeling. My body relaxed, and I really got into the mood. This strange but

great feeling took over me, and I went in eat-a-bitch-up mode. Like never before, I latched onto her and looped my arms under her legs, leaving fingerprints in her thighs, I ate her like never before. Nene's pussy tasted good, and her pre-nut was thin but sweet. Somehow my senses were taking me deeper into the art of entertainment. A beast broke out in me on stage, and I was really enjoying the mood. I gave no more thought to the man taking me hard, because whenever I wiggled my ass a little, he would pop it and grind me harder. The rough sex hurt a little at first, but now I felt no pain.

My focus became solely on the pussy in front of me. Slowly it came to mind how she used to look at me a little funny, and now I was in position to make her pay and make her want what she wished she had. Taking one pussy lip at a time, I pulled on it and rubbed my tongue inside that side, and like I thought, she tried to run. But it was too late; she was locked, and if she moved before I finished, Mrs. Lee would have her ass on the chopping block. I snarled at Nene, and she lay back down to take these speech instructions I was writing inside of her. Trying to figure out what she liked, I tried all kinds of mouth methods to make her move her ass. It seemed as though sucking her clit hard, and then sticking my face deep in her pussy was the thing. When I discovered her hot spot, I used it to my advantage and made her try to run. She started putting the pussy where I could get it, and every so often I would

intentionally bite her clit, not enough to make her holla, but enough to give her pleasure. NeNe started grinding her ass on the carpet, as I drove my tongue deep into her pussy.

To my surprise, she began to moan and grunt, then I allowed the rough rider to hold my hands as they were stretched back towards him, leaving only my head to dangle between her legs. Each time he would bang me hard, I would peck at her pussy with my tongue inside her. The crowd was going wild and so was NeNe, and without warning, she tightened her legs around my neck and her ass was off the ground. I used her move to eat away at her pretty-ass pussy. Maybe it was the pill or a new freak being reborn in me, but I tried to swallow her up and she started to tremble and jump. Those juices were mine. I cared not if it was all over me, but I had to let her recognize that I was the bad bitch, she needed to get on my team or get the fuck off the field.

At this time, the Rough Rider let my hands become free, and I pulled NeNe deeper into my face. She couldn't take it, but I made that bitch take it, and like many others, she, too, pleaded for me to stop. I let my head rise up, and then stared back. The crowd went out of control because they were seeing firsthand how a freaky bitch handled a dirty-ass bitch. NeNe was weak and her legs felt like dead weight around my neck, but I could tell that she was pleased, because she could not move. When I dropped them to the

stage area, she lay there out of it, but I wasn't finished. Before I could start on her again, the Rough Rider came into the condom.

When he pulled out of me, I got on my back and placed my head between his legs while he was taking off the condom. Showing no mercy, I started sucking his balls, putting them both in my mouth. The Rough Rider's body started tensing up and he froze, but he started shooting more nuts everywhere, and this time it was all over my breasts and running down to the carpet. With the extra nut on my breasts, I started sexually rubbing it inside my skin. When the Rough Rider fell back, I looked into the crowd, using my index finger to rub it up. Without warning, I placed the leftover nut into my mouth and pretended it was a hearty dick, sucking on my finger as if it was a real dick. As NeNe and I were being lowered to the bottom, the crowd was still going wild over the flick they saw firsthand, and all I could hear coming out of Mrs. Lee's mouth was, "Yes. Yes. Yes, you are a bad-ass bitch, a real moneymaker."

Mr. Lee came over, and he looked even happier than his wife. He said, "You were looking like a real stallion out there. You have blown quite a few minds out there tonight."

"Thanks," I spoke, not knowing what else to say. My eyes were feeling so tight. My high seemed liked it boosted more as I stopped moving. NeNe jumped off the stage and ran to the back of the

dressing room. She acted like I did her wrong, but I didn't tell her to put her pussy on my pussy plate.

"Girl, you are the perfect candidate. Damn, I'm so glad you are here. The club has taken in at least ten thousand dollars tonight. That's not including what Dawn has paid me for you," she spoke.

"I still have to go with her?" I spoke, feeling groggy.

"Yes. She has paid for you. Bitch, don't start this bullshit with me now. I need that extra five thousand dollars," she spoke while helping me off the stage.

Dave walked over and picked me up into his arms. Mrs. Lee and Mr. Lee walked behind us as he took me to the bathroom. They both walked back inside the club, not saying anything else.

"Are you all right?" Dave asked, while holding my face to look at him.

"Yes. I just see two of you," I spoke.

"Damn. You knew better than to take that shit NeNe gave you. She's popping all kinds of pills. I don't know what the fuck she gave you."

"It's all good Dave. I will be all right."

"Yeah, I know. I just don't want you to be like these pill-popping whores around here. Those bitches are taking a little bit of everything. You need to watch out and be aware. Don't take shit from them."

"Okay. This is a lesson learned," I spoke, as I tried to stand up.

"Come on and take a shower. You need to have a level head when Dawn takes you home."

"Yeah, I know."

Dave looked at me and walked me into the bathroom in the office. He helped me pull off my clothes and I took a long shower. Dave stood outside the door until I was finished. After the shower, I felt a little better. I was still groggy, but better. I got dressed and walked out to meet Dawn.

"Are you ready to ride?" she spoke with this manly voice.

"Sure. I'm ready," I spoke, as I swallowed.

"Okay. I don't have all night," she spoke, as she began walking out of the club.

I followed her out to her car. Dave jumped in the Tahoe and followed us. She was quiet the entire time we were riding. It was good, because it gave me a chance to lay my head back and relax. As I felt my body begin to relax, the car stopped. I held up my head and saw that we were at the hotel where I stayed. She got out and I followed. Locking her car doors, she walked over to me and grabbed me by the hand. I was looking around for Dave. I didn't see him anywhere. This shit didn't look good; he said he would be there for me. Yet his ass was nowhere around.

We rode the elevator to the third floor. I stayed on the fifth floor of the hotel. Arriving at Room 345, she swiped the keycard to enter. We walked through the door and Dawn went straight to the

bathroom. I closed the door and watched for a few seconds as she began to undress. Following her lead, I began undressing also. As she undressed, she said, "I have something to tell you, and I don't know how you will take it."

"Okay, what is it?" I said.

"Get in the bed first, if you don't mind."

Since she was paying me for tonight, I obeyed her. As soon as I started to get in the bed, my cell rang; it was Mrs. Lee.

I looked at Dawn and she replied, "Answer it."

Picking up the phone, I replied, "Yes, I am busy. What do you want?"

She was rambling on like a jealous pimp in my ear, and I most definitely wasn't feeling it or her like that. It was like she forgot that that I was being paid to do a job, which meant I didn't have time for this shit. Right then, I saw I had to be careful with letting her taste my goods, because she was losing her damn mind.

Acting as if I could not hear her, I replied, "Hey boss lady, I have to go, we can chat later. Bye."

Placing my phone on silent, I laid on my back and Dawn said, "Look at this and tell me what you think."

She pulled her robe off, and I could not hold it in. "Oh, hell no!" I jumped up out of the bed and reached for my clothes.

"You whore around and look at me like I have a disease."

What she said did make sense, but I still felt funny about getting in the bed with her. I responded to her, "What are you expecting from me? 'Cause you have both and you only paid for one service. Does Mrs. Lee know of your double pleasure?"

Dawn looked away and then replied, "No."

"What do you mean that Mrs. Lee does not know that you are a hermaphrodite?" I asked.

"Christina, let this be our secret and let me have you every now and then. What you say?"

"Cash is king, and if you want me quiet, pay for it."

"A one-time fee?" she asked.

"Yeah, a one-time fee."

She walked over to her purse and wrote me a check. I saw that it was for ten thousand. Putting my eyes on her, I said, "Who the fuck you think you are trying to bribe? I'm not a cheap-broke bitch. You better add some more numbers."

She tore the check up and wrote another one for twenty thousand dollars. I looked at it and said, "If this mutherfucking check bounces, so will your head on my fist. Are we clear?"

"Yes."

As she got into bed, she pushed my arm, telling me to turn over on my left side. I lay on my side as she wrapped her arms around me. She kissed and kissed the back of my neck, until she fell asleep. No sex. No licking. No ramming the dildo in her. I was

disappointed, but I fell asleep too. Fuck it; this was her money, plus I needed to get my mind right, and if she wanted to sleep, then fine with me.

Chapter 13

Waking up that morning, I moved away from Dawn. She took her arm off me and I got up. Rushing to put on my clothes, I fell over. I jumped up to see if I had awakened her, but she continued to sleep. I grabbed all of my things and rushed out. That was one strange bitch. As I jumped on the elevator and headed up to my hotel room on the fifth floor, I heard one of the doors open. I jumped back, hoping that it wasn't Dawn. The doors closed and I let out a long sigh. *I've encountered a lot of things, but a hermaphrodite has never been one of them*, I thought while putting my hand over my forehead and bending over. I began to feel a little dizzy. It's probably because I hadn't eaten. Don't know what it was, but this was a fucked up feeling.

Finally, sitting on the bed, I decided to call Peaches to come over and help me. That pill had me sick to my stomach. As I lifted

145

the cell phone to call Peaches, the phone began to ring, and it was Paris. What the fuck does this bitch want with me?

"What do you want?" I spoke over the phone.

"I'm checking on you to see if you were okay. We all know that NeNe slipped you a roofie. She was being a bitch. I still care, Christina," she spoke.

"Bitch, I can't tell you still care. You acting like one of the scandalous-ass mutherfuckers we always had to deal with. You are no better than the rest of them, treating me like a fucking stranger."

"I'm sorry. Do you forgive me?" she asked.

"Bitch. I don't know what you have planned. You could be setting me up for all I know. You have fucking changed, and I don't want no part of it," I stated, while hanging the phone up in her face. Fuck Paris. That bitch will pay. We have been friends for years, and now she acting like a real whore. Fuck her and all the haters that are associated with her.

As I looked down at my phone, it began to vibrate. Paris was calling me back-to-back like she was fucking me. I really didn't want to talk to her right now. She had disappointed me, and I didn't want to feel that way again. Friends stand by each other, not stab them in the back.

Lying back on the bed, I put my cell on vibrate. I really got tired of hearing it ring back-to-back to back. This bitch really wants me to curse her ass out.

I closed my eyes to relax; my stomach began to bubble. I jumped up, running to the bathroom. Vomit was coming up out of my nose and my mouth. This shit had me really sick. When I went back to the club, I was going to beat NeNe's ass or she was going to beat mine. This bitch has got to be taught a lesson.

After I finished vomiting, I called Peaches, and now she was headed over to help me get over this shit. I had to be ready by Saturday night. I was going home, fuck this. This is good for Mrs. Lee to keep me in a hotel, but I miss my apartment. At least Pete, Peaches, or the kids came by to see me. Over here, nothing is popping off.

Finally, Peaches showed up. I had never been so happy to see anyone in my life. Her face lit up so bright, like a full moon on a pleasant night.

"I'm so glad to see you, Peaches. I feel like shit," I explained to her.

"What's going on with you?"

"This girl slipped me a pill, and I've been sick to my stomach ever since. When I see her again, I'm going to beat the brakes off her ass. This bitch is playing with my life. Suppose that pill would have killed me?"

"Yeah, you are right. She could have killed you, but thank God you are alive," Peaches stated.

"I guess so. Well, I'm ready to go. Carry that bag out."

We headed out of the hotel room and into the car. Peaches had this weird look on her face. She looked sicker than I did. Even though her face glowed, she looked sick. Like something was bothering her.

"What's wrong with you, Peaches?" I asked.

"I have something to tell you, but I don't want to get into it just now."

"Well tell me, I am listening," I said, trying to sound as sincere as possible, but I honestly felt horrible.

Peaches looked at me, dropped her head and replied, "Nothing, I just don't feel well right now."

"And why is that? Don't tell me that Pete has done something stupid. Has he hit you?" I asked, almost ready to go off.

"No, he hasn't hit me. He just hasn't touched me."

"You mean he hasn't fucked you?"

"It's not all about Peter, and he has not fucked me yet. I mean, I would love for him to come home for once and make love to me, or at least tell me that he loves me. He doesn't do anything anymore. Just eats and goes to sleep. He's getting to the point where he doesn't play with the kids either."

"Well, fuck Pete. We have each other. I will take care of you, if that's what you like," I spoke.

"I just feel that you should know that I have left my girlfriend alone."

"I thought I was your only girlfriend," I said in an angry way, because no one fucks with bitches I care about.

"Christina, you are now, but I know you have others, and I get lonely when you are gone, so when I am in the mood for pussy, I go to her."

"I see," were the only words I could say.

"I feel bad about it, but I felt you should know."

"Who is this other bitch that you been seeing?" I spoke, getting angrier by the thought of her with another woman. I had never really given a fuck about my bitches. But somehow Peaches had become more than that to me. She was my friend; my girlfriend, I guess. We hung out, and when needed, we took care of each other, like she was taking care of me right now.

She said, "She is someone I used to see. That means she is in the past."

"Fine, as long as there are no other ones but me, because you belong to me," I said in such a way that she knew that I was not playing, but I couldn't help it. I guess I had the mentality of a man and the double standard definitely applied here. I could do what I wanted, but I would definitely fuck Peaches up if I needed to.

"I would love that, Christina," Peaches replied with a big smile on her face.

We continued to ride home in peace. All types of things crossed my mind. I wanted to go to the club and put my foot in

NeNe's ass. That bitch had to pay for what she did. The more I thought about it, the more my stomach began to turn over. As soon as Peaches stopped the car, I opened the door and began throwing up badly. I threw up so much that I pissed a little on myself.

"Damn!" I yelled out.

"What's the matter?" Peaches asked, while running around the car to where I stood.

"Girl, I pissed on myself," I spoke while laughing.

"Pissed on yourself? Stop playing."

"I'm so serious, Peaches," I replied while holding onto the car, still bending over.

"Come on. Let's go inside before someone sees your wet ass," she joked.

"Girl, you are crazy," I spoke, laughing.

Peaches grabbed me around the waist and took me upstairs to my apartment. Opening the door, I could smell nothing but bleach.

"Damn Peaches, did you empty a whole bottle of bleach on the floor?"

"No, I just wanted everything to be sanitized before you came home," she replied.

"I have to admit, you did a perfect job."

"Thank you. Go ahead and prepare the tub while I fix you a glass of milk to help settle your stomach."

I didn't hesitate. I just walked towards the bathroom and ran a tub filled with hot water. I stripped off my clothes and sat down to relax myself once again. I closed my eyes.

"Here you go," Peaches spoke as she handed me the small glass of milk.

"Thank you so much. I really appreciate you. You know how to take care of your friends."

"Yes I do. Especially a friend like you," she replied with a smile big enough to show off her cute dimples.

I drank the glass of milk and relaxed some more. It felt so good to be back at home. As I sat in the tub soaking, the thought of Peaches' soft body against mine played in my head. I licked my lips; I wanted to taste her now.

"Peaches," I yelled out.

"Yes, baby?" she replied.

"Come get in the tub with me."

"Anything for you, baby."

Peaches began stripping slowly. My nipples began to get very hard, and I glided my index fingers over them with soap dripping off. She stood there completely naked, leaning against the marble counter. Rising out of the tub, I got on the floor and crawled up to her, looking seductive. Peaches spread her legs and I began kissing her on her thighs, and moving up to her purring pussy. Parting her lips to look at her clit, I rubbed my finger gently over her. She

began to sing low moans of happiness. I stuck my finger at the beginning of her hole, then glided deeper inside. Peaches let out more cries as I began to lick her, until she nutted right there in my face. It didn't take long for her to cum. She must really be horny.

I continued to eat her pussy until she came once more, letting me know that she really wanted to be fucked. After that, we finished our shower together and I proceeded to put on my strap-on. He was a good nine inches, and Peaches loved it. She could handle that dick pounding against her walls.

Laying Peaches on the bed, I began tasting her again until I was ready to dig deep. She rose up, licking my nipples as I caressed her breasts too. Pushing her back onto the bed, I fiddled with her pussy again, and then entered her. She was so wet and slippery. I worked it for about five seconds and I was in the gate. Peaches moaned louder and louder, and I pounded that fucking pussy. My dildo was solid black, but the more I fucked Peaches, it turned white, dripping with cum. She really needed this fuck.

I watched as her body began shaking; as more nut poured out her pussy. Just to see the expression on her face made my pussy throw up with cum. My body quivered until I was finished. That was the hardest nut I had ever spit out. I collapsed right there on the bed next to Peaches. She turned over, looking at me.

"Why are you staring at me like that?" I asked.

"No reason. I guess you knew exactly what I needed."

"Yes, I know your body."

"You are so special, Christina, and I do love you," she replied.

"Love. Girl, what do you know about love?" I asked with a smile.

"I know a lot about love. And the way you make me feel. How you go out of your way to make me and my kids happy. I know it has to be love," Peaches explained.

"I see," I spoke as I got off the bed and proceeded to the bathroom to clean up.

I took a short shower and got dressed. As I came back into the room, I saw that Peaches sat there naked with her head in her hands. I knew she wanted me to say I love her; but damn, not now. I don't want her to think I'm going to leave Pierre for her. She and her kids can come along with us, but I'm not leaving him.

"What's wrong now, Peaches? You know that I love your black ass. Don't go soft on me now. What do you want me to do?" I asked.

"I just want to be loved. And I feel like you are the one to love me."

"I do love you, but what about Pete? What are you planning on doing with him?"

"Pete doesn't love me. He hasn't loved me for years. He only puts up with me because you are around. You're the main reason we are still married," she explained.

"Well, I guess when I go back to Mississippi, you and the kids will live with me. There is only one problem. I have Pierre," I spoke.

"I know, Christina," Peaches said while letting out a low laugh.

"I sure as hell can't tell him that my girlfriend and her kids want to move in with us. He would probably kill me. But I will tell him that you and the kids will move with us. As soon as I tell him I will move in with him, he won't care who else moves in."

"Really. Me as your girlfriend?"

"Yes, you are my girlfriend. Ever since I tasted your sweet pussy, you belong to me. Fuck Pete. He will be all right. Just know that Pierre and I will be married one day, but I love you too. Don't ever forget that," I spoke.

"I love you too, Christina," Peaches spoke, as she hugged me passionately.

"Good, now get dressed and start packing. I will leave and go back home at the end of July. Do you really want to come with me?"

"Hell yeah, I do. You make me feel so damn good."

I knew she was very excited if she was cursing. Peaches didn't curse unless she was made to or excited. I replied, "Well, it's official. You are moving back to Mississippi with me and Pierre."

Peaches got dressed and headed across the hall to her apartment, waiting on the kids to come home. I wanted her to make

sure they had a home-cooked meal every day. Opening the refrigerator, I took out the Red Beans & Rice that Peaches had prepared for me. As I sat at the table, my mind was focused on Saturday. I had to be prepared for Saturday night. Mrs. Lee told me that two men, Dennis Dawson and Kevin Jones, had reserved me. All types of thoughts ran through my head. What do they have in store for me? Probably double penetration or one fucking me, while I sucked the other's dick. Whatever it was, I knew these two mutherfuckers were probably going to give me a hard time.

Chapter 14

Dave came by to pick me up early. I wanted to go to the club and confront NeNe about that mutherfucking pill. I didn't tell anyone I would be coming. because they would have tried to stop me, and there's nothing like the element of surprise. *This bitch will have to boot up or shut the fuck up*, I thought as I remembered how sick I was over that pill.

I walked in the club, not even speaking to anyone. My focus was on the locker room in the back where we all meet up. Dave saw me and instantly knew what I was about to do, so he rushed behind me. A few more of the club members rushed behind him, trying to see what was going on, because Dave moved like a skilled warrior. I walked up to the door of the dressing room, and Paris was walking out the door. She saw the expression on my face

and ran inside, locking the door behind her, because she knows me too well and she knows when I am pissed, I am pissed.

"Bitch, open this damn door now and wait your turn! As for now, I will handle NeNe and you later," I said fiercely.

"If you go in there trying to fight NeNe, the rest of them will jump you. And I can't have that bullshit go down. You are still my girl, even if we have our beef. Fuck whatever that dumb shit is, and keep your mind on that paper."

"Bitch, I'm not thinking about what your trifling ass is saying right now. I know you must be in on this 'Let's get Christina shit', so right damn now, open the fucking door and let me deal with who the fuck ever, if it's not you."

Before I could kick the door, she opened it and starting saying, "Christina, I can't let you fight, listen to me, I can't let you..."

Before Paris could get finish the rest of her sentence, I slapped that bitch right in her fucking face. "Bitch, I said step."

Paris looked stunned that I hit her ass, because all she could yell was, "Christy!" If she had some balls, she would have got down and ugly with me, but she knows me, and it's "Fuck a bitch up season."

Stepping close to her, I replied, "Don't fuck with me! I'm so tired of all this bullshit from all you hoes. Ever since I got here, you have been nothing but fucking trouble. Mainly you, my supposed–to–be friend. We were to stick with each other, not go

behind each other's back talking slick shit," I stated, as I pushed her out of the way.

Opening the door, Nene was standing there looking good, wearing her matching bra and panty set. She was sitting on the stool looking into the mirror when I came in. Nene turned towards me, and when she saw the look on my face, her countenance fell. I thought, *I don't want to fight her, but she has to pay for what the fuck she did to me.* I could only see red, and not beautiful NeNe. With anger inside of me, my mind state was, *Kick ass now, and talk about it later.* Walking as fast as I could, I didn't ask any questions, because a bitch came to take care of business.

She didn't have a chance to get all the way up, because I flew right into her, throwing punches. I grabbed her hair and wrapped it around in my hand. She tripped and fell to the floor. I pulled and pulled her fucking hair, until some came out in my hand. Jumping down on her, I kept punching and punching that bitch in the face. We were going toe-to-toe, and I must admit that bitch was taking that ass-kicking in style. I got off her and started stomping her in the floor, until Dave ran over and picked me up off her. I began yelling, "Let me go! I'm so tired of you bitches running around this mutherfucking place hating."

"Calm down," Dave spoke while dragging me out of the locker room. Cherry and Chocolate ran over, helping NeNe off the floor. She pushed them out of the way trying to get at me. NeNe pushed

me right in the fucking face, and Cherry grabbed her again. Dave let me go and we were back at it again. This time Cherry was trying to fight me and Paris jumped in it, fighting her. We all were throwing blows until....

"Bitches, have y'all lost your fucking minds?" Mrs. Lee yelled out, as she looked at the entire environment of bitches scrapping and blood scratches.

Dave grabbed me. Chocolate grabbed NeNe. Mr. Lee separated Cherry and Paris. We all were fucked up with a little blood here and a few scratches there.

"Which one of you bitches started this shit? I mean right damn now. Which one of you started this shit? Come on out with it," Mr. Lee spoke, looking all buff and shit.

"I did," I spoke as I yanked my arm away from Dave to walk over to Mrs. Lee. The other females looked at each other. I saw Paris shaking her head from side to side, hoping to go unnoticed.

"What's the fucking problem, Christina? There is no fighting in my club. Never. And since you can't control yourself, you will have to be punished," she spoke.

"Well, I don't give a fuck. This bitch gave me a pill and could have killed me."

"That pill wasn't going to do shit to you but help relax you," Mrs. Lee spoke in a calmer tone.

"So you knew she was going to slip me that fucking pill? The same pill that made me sick?"

"I'm the one who told her to give it to you" Mrs. Lee said in my face.

"You don't know what effect that pill would have had on me. Suppose I was pregnant and you have bitches slipping me pills and shit!" I yelled. Before I could say anything else, Mrs. Lee slapped the shit out of me.

Before she walked off, Mrs. Lee said, "Don't you ever call me a bitch again. I'm your boss; you are not mine. Now, you bitches get cleaned up for tonight. Christina, I will meet you in my office. NOW!"

Instead of me going to her office like she told me, I went to the bar to get a vodka and Coke. I need a fucking drink. *I'll kill this bitch*, I thought as I sipped on my drink. She was very lucky I didn't hit her ass back. I downed that drink and took another one to the head.

"Christina, are you all right?" Paris spoke as she approached me with more caution.

"Yes, I am. Are you?"

"Yes."

"So what was that supposed to prove, that we are friends again? That you are down with me again? Paris, you've made me feel like I'm shit since I have been here. Friends don't treat each

160

other like that. I love you, girl, and you turned your back on me," I spoke.

"Christy, don't say that. It should have proven a lot. I'm down with you in whatever you do."

"I believe you in a way. You just surprised me with all this bullshit."

"I'm sorry, Christy. How can I make it up to you?" she asked.

"Well, we can hang out tomorrow. I hear that my night won't be long. About five hours," I stated.

"Who are you going up with tonight?"

"Some guys named Kevin and Dennis."

"Kevin and Dennis? Hell naw! You don't need to fuck them two. We all have had a terrible experience with them two fools, and it wasn't nice. Tell Mrs. Lee that you can't do it," she stated.

"If I don't, she will fire me. Shit, I'm probably already fired," I replied.

"She won't fire you. Her and Damien were already talking about taking you home with them. She might curse you out, but not fire you. She needs you. Too many of her clients have seen you, and trust me, baby girl, they want you," Paris spoke, while lifting the glass to her mouth and taking a drink.

"I don't think I can back out of this."

"If you can't, then bring plenty of liquor or take another pill, because you're going to need it."

"I will drink liquor, but I'm not taking another pill. That shit had my head swimming."

"Okay, then drink up," Paris spoke, as she looked around and saw Mrs. Lee staring at her. She finished her drink and moved on to another spot in the club. Mrs. Lee stood there with her hand on her hips. I finished my drink, then walked over to her. As I passed her, she gave me a push into the office door.

"Bitch, you're going to make me go off on you. You need to get in line," she spoke while walking over to her chair and the wooden desk.

"I will, as soon as your bitches fall in line and leave me alone. You see what's going on, and these whores don't give a fuck about what you say."

"They care; they pretend in front of you. I will deal with them later. It's all about you now."

"Well, am I fired or what? Do I need to get my shit and go?" I rudely asked.

"Hell no, you're not fired. Why would you think that?"

"I just guessed. Didn't know what was on your mind. You did slap me."

"That was to get your fucking attention. Sometimes you don't listen. Just running your trap and not paying attention."

"Whatever."

"Yeah, whatever. You just be ready tonight for Kevin and Dennis. They are paying me $50,000 for you for five hours. And you better not misbehave," she demanded.

"Well, I hope they don't misbehave; then I won't have to get ugly."

"You better do whatever they tell you to do," she spoke.

"If you say so."

"Christina, get the fuck out of my office and get ready to go. Dave will drop you off at their house. Just fuck and behave. Be a good girl for once," she replied.

"Don't think I can be," I smiled and walked out shaking my ass. I stopped at the door and started making my ass cheeks jump one at a time.

"Get your ass out of here," Mrs. Lee spoke while throwing some paper.

I closed the door and walked over to the bar. The bartender gave me three more drinks and I was on my way with Dave. We drove for almost an hour. Around this time, I was so gone. My head began to spin and shit.

Finally we pulled up at this blue house with white shutters. There was this cute mutherfucking man standing on the outside. He was light-skinned, clean shaven, and had magnificent white teeth with a nice church appeal about him. He had on a white shirt, a black tie, and slacks. *If you look at him, you would not think that*

he was into the shit I am about to put on but then again, you wouldn't think I am like that either if you looked at me, I thought as my eyes soaked up my environment around me. As soon as I got out, Dave drove off like a bat out of hell. I thought Mrs. Lee said he would be standing on the outside waiting on me; this nigga took off with the wheels wailing. *Now I am really nervous*, I thought as I proceeded up towards the steps.

The closer I got, the more his eyes scanned me all over, and he yelled, "The pussy is here!" When I walked past him, this nigga snatched me from the back and put a chokehold on my neck. My smile faded to a surprised frown, because I was totally caught off-guard by this rough shit. He kicked the front door open and took me inside. The other guy was brown-skinned with moles in his face. The fucker was ugly, and in fact he was the worst one I had encountered since arriving to this town. He looked nasty, and the room didn't look clean at all. I thought, *What the hell has Mrs. Lee signed me up for?* The church boy's hands were still around me, while the ugly fucker was standing on top of the table dancing. The song *Set It Off*, by Lil Boosie was ringing out, and he looked too rowdy for me. When he let me go, he said, "I'm Kevin, and that is Dennis there on the table; we going to fuck you so hard. Damn, you're fine. Better than the rest of the bitches that have come over here," he stated.

If you could be fooled by appearances alone, I surely was. Then Kevin pushed me in Dennis's direction. He jumped off the table and ran into me, knocking me onto the floor and knocking the breath out of me. Kevin undressed, while Dennis dropped his pants and ordered me to put his dick in my mouth. I sat on the side of the bed, bent my head down, and saw his dick. To my dismay, I wanted to laugh; it would add injury to insult if I did, but I couldn't help it. I grinned; the dick was short, hairy and fat. *I could handle this nigga*, I thought, but it had a slight smell of alcohol, cologne, and sweat.

Dennis got down between my legs and stuck his nasty-ass fingers in my pussy. I wanted to get angry, because his fingers had black dirt in the nails and he had oil on his hands. At least Kevin was cleaner, but he kept touching my back, so I pretended that I was in a faraway place just to take my mind off these nasty fuckers in the room. With my attention going back to Dennis, he was rough, and the nigga didn't even loosen me up. He kept trying to finger-fuck me, but he couldn't do it right. I reached down and pulled his contaminated hand out of my aching pussy. Kevin saw me and began choking me, saying, "Bitch, we are running the show, not you. We paid to have your fine ass here. So leave us the fuck alone."

Barely talking, I faintly spoke the words, "Well, that shit hurt. If either one of you hadn't shown discourtesy, I would be acting better and thrill the fuck out you both."

"Choke that bitch some more," Dennis called out to Kevin.

Since Kevin was behind me, it was easy for him to clasp his hands around my neck and put pressure on me. I tried to get his hands away from my neck, but he was very stout. Kevin grabbed both of my hands until I almost fainted, and seeing my eyes roll backwards, he let me go before I could pass all the way out. I could feel my body sliding to the floor. They lifted me on the couch and put me on my back, while Dennis rammed dick inside of me. He was bouncing back and forward like in a rocking chair, only it was on my pussy. Kevin grabbed my chin while holding his dick and shoved his cologne-dick in my mouth. I began sucking what I could, because spit rolled down my jaws and the smell was horrible. If I could run away and not come back, I would have, but they have paid to play and it's me they are playing with.

A few minutes went by and they switched up. Neither one of them hurt me, because they were short and fat. The foreplay was bad. I expected one to be long, but not two short, fat dicks trying to fuck me. That's probably why they fucked rough, because they were shamed. Deep down, I laughed to myself.

Kevin jumped out of my pussy fast and flipped me over. He bent me over the couch. Dennis went around to the back and put

more dick in my throat. Kevin was trying to go in my ass, and I kept moving around. Dennis moved back and began choking me, while Kevin rammed his dick in my ass. I tried to yell out but couldn't, because I was being choked out. He fucked and fucked until he thought my ass was loose.

Finally, Dennis loosened his hands around my neck and put his dick back in my mouth. I tried to suck, but my ass was burning. I was used to anal sex, but not like this. This nigga didn't even put KY Jelly on. He just rammed my pussy and jabbed at my ass. In a way, it felt good.

They switched up and Dennis was gentler. He put KY Jelly on my ass, while slapping my ass cheeks. "I'm not ramming dick in her like that, scratching up my head," he spoke.

"Nigga, my dick isn't scratched up. That shit felt good to hear her scream like a little bitch for me to stop," Kevin replied.

Finally, after that position, I began to ride Dennis like a cow girl. Kevin poured more KY Jelly on my ass and entered me. I stopped moving so he could penetrate my ass. There it was; me being double penetrated by the two. *If only they were longer and gentler*, I thought. They fucked and fucked until they came. Kevin was first then Dennis. I got up to get my clothes, because I was past ready to leave this dump. When someone tapped me on the shoulder, I turned around and Kevin punched me in the face. I fell to the floor, knocked out.

Someone dashed water in my face. Waking up, I realized I couldn't move. Opening my eyes, I saw that I was tied down at a small wooden table and my knees were placed in a chair. Rope covered my body. "What the fuck is going on here?" I screamed out.

"Bitch, shut the fuck up! You about to get fucked good before you leave this mutherfucker," Kevin spoke.

"Untie me right now, you little dick bastard."

"Little. How about I pour some dick into your little ass?" he spoke, as he came around the table and began fucking me in the ass. I began to yell out and he put his right hand over my mouth. "Shut up, bitch. You want to be fucked, don't you? See how a little dick can make you yell?"

He stroked and stroked harder, trying to get that nut. Just before he came, he stopped. Dennis came over and began fucking my ass. He stroked slower, but it still hurt. Kevin went and brought back a purple dildo. He began shoving it in my mouth like he was trying to break my teeth. When I wouldn't do what he wanted me to, he began slapping me in the face with it. To them it felt good to take my body like that. I didn't know that pain could feel so good. Finally, these jackasses untied me. Their time had ended, and neither one of them apologized for their stupid behavior.

"Get your clothes, bitch, and get the fuck out!" Kevin yelled, as he threw my clothes out the door.

"I will. You two niggas need to grow bigger dicks and learn tips in fucking," I spoke. as I began to exit the door. Kevin came over and kicked me out the door onto the porch. I fell down and looked back at that asshole. He smiled and slammed the door in my face.

I got dressed and sat there on the porch waiting for Dave to show up. Fifteen minutes went by, and he finally pulled up. I walked off and looked back at the house. Dennis was standing in the window. I flipped that nigga off and jumped in the vehicle. He mooned me and closed the curtain.

Looking over at Dave, I demanded, "Where the fuck was you?"

"I had to run back to the club for a minute. Mrs. Lee wanted me to go on a run for her."

"What the fuck was she thinking, sending me over to these two short psychotic dick mutherfuckers?"

"What happened? All the girls have complained about them two, but she keeps sending girls over to them. What did they do to you? What happened to your face and throat?"

"It's not even important anymore, 'cause you weren't there for me like you were supposed to be. Take me back to the club!" I yelled while looking out the window.

Dave looked at me and then drove off. Deep down, something told me to keep all that shit to myself. I was too embarrassed to tell anyone what them mutherfuckers did. The other girls already

knew. I'm glad Paris warned me, even though I didn't believe her. It never crossed my mind that these fucks would be this wild. I know one thing. These bitches won't get me back over here again. Fuck that, I thought they were going to kill me choking me out and shit. Fucking psychos!

Chapter 15

"Mrs. Lee, what the hell were you thinking when you sent me over there?" I spoke with an attitude.

"What happened? Did they treat you like a queen?" she replied, being sarcastic.

"You know them fuckers are crazy. What were you thinking?"

"If they did anything wrong, I will talk to them," she said until she saw my face.

"Talk to them? You must be shitting me? Ha! You know what? Don't worry about it; I refuse to go back over there fucking off with them two clowns. They need some help. Seriously, and I need some rest, so I'm taking some days off. I don't need Dave for his whack-ass protection or driving. My fucking throat is sore, my face is bruised, and I just need some time to myself."

"Well, it's over with, Christina. I want you to come home with Mr. Lee and me. We want to take you to our home and show you how we love."

"Why me?" I asked.

"Because you're special to me," Mrs. Lee said, with a deranged look on her face. "I always get what I want, and I want you."

"You got that fire," Mr. Lee jumped in.

Mrs. Lee looked at her husband and spoke softly," Let me have a word alone with Christina."

He did not exchange words, but left like an obedient child.

"Christina, let's put all the cards on the table and be honest."

"What are you getting at, Mrs. Lee?"

"You and I, that is what I am getting at. Can't you tell by the way I act that I want you?"

"No actually, I thought you did all the newbies like that."

Walking off from me, she replied loudly, "Hell no! They are clean, but not good enough for me. You are the one I taste and the one I plan to take to my house for good. I will always have you, and you will always have me. In time you will see."

"Does Mr. Lee know of your intentions?" I asked.

"I run him, and don't worry about that. You will be pleased with both of us, you will be only mine. It's only right that I take care of you and treat you how you deserve to be treated."

Laughing, I shook my head, because I was stunned that my boss wanted a down low relationship with me.

"Do you know how many of them would love to have this opportunity?"

"I do, but I don't want a relationship with you."

She did not reply, she simply brushed me off and called for her husband to come back in.

Mrs. Lee bowed her head to him and motioned for me to hug her. I gave her a hug, and she cuffed my ass. Whispering in my ear, "I can't wait to have you to myself, tasting you all night for many days to come."

I looked into her eyes and she kissed me passionately. My response was to kiss her back. Our tongues explored each other for a few minutes, until Mr. Lee cleared his throat. Mrs. Lee pulled back, and we began to laugh at each other. I'm sure we were laughing for different reasons, but she would never know that.

As I walked out of the office, he spanked me on the ass. I continued to walk towards the locker room to fix my face, at least a little to hide the visible bruising. Someone was going to pay for those bastards fucking me up like that. After I made myself as normal-looking as possible, I headed to the bar. My good feeling had worn off. These fools would kill anyone's high. I sat down at the bar; the bartender fixed me a drink. I had a martini on the rocks, as I looked at the stage and saw Cherry shaking that ass. She

was dancing so hard it made me want to taste that pussy. Damn, that bitch knew how to shake it. She was dropping that ass like Paris. I got so excited, I went to the front of the stage where the rest of the niggas sat. I took out my dollars; I wanted to play with that pussy too. They danced all around me. She knew why I was standing there. The bodyguards were stopping all those other niggas; fuck that, I went up on stage.

As soon as Cherry took off her bottom and laid flat on the floor, I crawled up on stage. A nigga tried to follow me, but the bodyguard stopped him. She was on the floor making her ass cheeks jump. I immediately got down and began licking her almond joy. Damn, that shit was the bomb. Lick after lick, I stuck my fingers in gently. I moved my famous tongue back and forward for a few minutes, and she came right there in front of everyone. After Cherry came, she jumped up, grabbed her clothes, and ran off stage. The DJ changed the songs while I stood up and bowed my head. The bodyguards helped me off the stage. Mrs. Lee was staring at me like she was ready to beat my ass. I just wanted a taste. It was looking too good up there, rocking and jiggling like that.

After a few more drinks, Mrs. Lee, Mr. Lee, and I headed to their house. We pulled up to a huge-ass house that looked like Pierre's house. The black gates opened, and we proceeded on. As the vehicle stopped, he walked over to my side of the vehicle and

picked me up. He carried me into the house like we were newlyweds. Mrs. Lee opened the door and walked behind us.

The lights were dim. Mrs. Lee took me to a shower in the guest bedroom. She and Mr. Lee took a shower together. It was strange that I didn't get a chance to take one with them, but they were a strange couple anyway.

Finally, we all gathered in the living room. Mrs. Lee had on a red silk teddy and Mr. Lee wore red silk shorts. They laid out a white silk teddy just for me. She took my hand and led me out on the balcony. Mr. Lee left and went to the kitchen. We sat down next to this huge swimming pool. Mrs. Lee laid me down and began applying her hands all over me. I glanced up and he came in with a bowl. It was full of the sticky fruit that was served at the club. Small drops then huge drops fell upon my skin as he poured the filling on me. Mrs. Lee took her hands and began rubbing the scent into my skin. He stepped to the right side of me and dropped to his knees, while Mrs. Lee stayed on the left. They kissed each other, and then they both began tasting me everywhere. His mouth was up high and her mouth was down low. It felt good having them take my body with such ease, especially after those two bastards mistreated me so badly. I couldn't believe they even wanted me with the way I was looking. It is my time now to be the most desired appetizer of the evening, and the way these two

carried on, it did not matter which I fucked first, as long as I got to fuck one.

Mrs. Lee told me to place my feet flat on the ground and I did. She rubbed the fruity syrup on my hot spot and began eating my pussy like a champion. Her long-ass tongue invaded me over and over again, pleasing me. She sucked my pussy lips, and I moaned with so much pleasure. Mrs. Lee was relaxing my body and making me feel too damn good. Then she began inserting her fingers one at a time inside my hole, stretching it and shaping it to her liking. Mrs. Lee sucked the syrup off me and said, "This is what I've been waiting to taste." Then she used her tongue to caress my pussy hole, and it took me away. I paid no attention to the fact that Mr. Lee stopped to get drinks, because I was in the mood for a woman, and as of now, I was already feeling tipsy and drunk as ever.

"Christina, I am not going to make you cum now. Let's go for a swim to cool off," Mrs. Lee said with syrup and pussy juice around her mouth.

We all took a few laps in the pool, and the water felt wonderful rushing over my skin and removing the sticky syrup from me. They led me inside, and this is where the real fucking began. He bent over and Mrs. Lee went to his backside, and began licking his ass. Her mouth found his balls as she picked them up one by one sucking. Her tongue invaded his ass, and he didn't yell out. Most

men would have stopped her, but he let her continue. This went on for about ten minutes, when Mrs. Lee waved for me to come with her. Mr. Lee lay out on this huge white bearskin rug.

"What's wrong?" I asked, not knowing what we were doing leaving him all alone.

"Here, put this on," she said as she handed me a black strapped dildo. The dildo attached was white and hers was a black dildo.

"I see. We are going to fuck each other while he watches."

"Just come on. You get in front while I go towards the back," she spoke as we walked back into the living room.

Me being dumb, it finally hit me. We are going to fuck Mr. Lee. OMG... And I thought this was all about me. This nigga wanted his wife to partner up with another female to fuck him. Damn it, boy!

All kind of ideas went through my head, and going with Mr. Lee was not one of them. *I should leave*, I thought as she stood in front of me. *What if I pretend to be sick or something?* I thought more, but the look in her eyes spoke of something strange. Sighing hard, I watched as Mrs. Lee bent down with the KY Jelly and spread it over his ass. She inserted it into him. I knelt down in front of him, and he began moaning and groaning, like a little bitch. He grabbed my strap on and began sucking out of control. Looking at him sucking that dick turned me on so bad. My pussy began aching

for dick. The more he sucked, the more I tried to shove the dildo down his throat.

Mrs. Lee and I switched positions. I got the KY Jelly and squirted it on his ass, then spread it with my hands. When I got the KY all over my hands I made a clapping sound, and like any bitch, he jumped then yelled out like a girl. Putting the dick to his ass, I slid it in slowly, and then began to rush, shoving deeper and deeper. I wanted him to yell out like Peaches. As I rammed him, Mrs. Lee got up and nodded for me to continue. I reached around and pulled his dick, as I moved slowly in and out. He grabbed his dick and began jacking himself off. I continued to fuck that nigga in the ass like no tomorrow. Finally, he busted that mutherfucking nut right there.

He got up and walked out afterwards. Mrs. Lee sat there on the couch stroking that dick like she wanted me to give her some.

"Take that thing off. I want to fuck you. Let me see if you can hold up to me fucking you."

"I can handle whatever you dish out."

"We will see. Now drop down on this dick and ride me," she spoke seductively.

I sat down on that dick and rode it. We kissed passionately. The kiss seemed like there were feelings of falling in love or something. I stopped and jumped up. Only Peaches got those types of kisses. This lady here was nobody but my boss.

"What's wrong with you?" she asked.

"I would rather you fuck me from the back. I want to feel everything you have to give me."

"I will give you that and more," she replied.

Bending over the couch, she slowly rammed dick inside me. I screamed out, but jumped back on that dick showing her how to work me. Her thumb slid into my ass, as she continued to fuck me. She fucked and fucked, and I gave out by putting nut on her dick.

Afterwards, I put Mrs. Lee on the floor and decided to make her pay for trying to take Peaches's place in my mind. As she opened up her legs, I touched the slender pussy with my hands. "You have a very nice-looking pussy and a nice smell," I said as I put my nose to it and continued, "It smells like lilac and roses. Has anyone ever told you that?" I said.

"Only few have ever been here and participated in tonight's event, and as for smelling this cunt, not many have," she said as she laid back.

I began licking her so she could get wetter, and she did. With my handy strap-on I entered her, and from the look on her face, it had been a long time since someone had entered her. She wrapped her legs around me and we humped together like lovers. She kept pulling me deeper into her, and I was allowing myself to sink into her lovely pussy hole. I was locked into her web of desire, as we fucked each other. Fucking a woman felt good, and the way she

wasn't cutting slack made me plunge deeper and deeper into her. Mrs. Lee put one of my breasts into her mouth and started scratching my back, as my arms lifted me up and down on her. She made me feel like a real stud, as I rocked her pussy around the room. Mrs. Lee stared into my eyes as we both came, and I didn't mind because she, like the rest, needed to know that when I am on the scene, I'm the bad bitch. After hours of fun, we collapsed on the floor as I rolled off her in exhaustion.

Later on that night, I woke up because I heard my cell phone go off. I looked around on the couch; Mrs. Lee had left me there. I walked over to the table and grabbed my purse. Looking at my cell phone, I saw that it was a message from Pierre. It read, "I'm on my way to Denver. What the fuck are you doing up there?"

I rubbed my face and shook my head. This nigga had lost his mind. I wondered what type of drama he had going on now. I would call him, but I was so fucking tired. I called Dave. He arrived and dropped me off at my apartment. It was five-thirty in the fucking morning. I was tired as fuck. Damn, I need a break from this freaky lifestyle I live, but the money was good, and freaking when I want was even better. How I was going to entwine the two, was anyone's best bet.

Chapter 16

When I crawled into bed, my body was aching for some R and R. I was there all day long. My cell phone was ringing off the hook. Shit, I was tired. After about the hundredth ring, I decided to answer the phone, and it was Mrs. Lee.

"What's up?"

"Girl, I have been trying to get ahold of you all day. Are you all right? We woke up and thought something had happened to you," she spoke in a panic.

"No. I came home and went to bed. I'm tired as a mutha."

"Well, you could have told someone where you were."

"Dave knew where I was; did you bother to ask him?"

"No, I didn't. We haven't seen him either. Well, get up and come down to the club. I have a huge surprise for you," she blurted out.

181

"What surprise?"

"Just come on. We have a taste test going on today just for you."

"A taste test. That doesn't sound too good. But I will be on. Give me about an hour. I thought today was for the men."

"Yes, it is for the men, but we will have a private meeting back in the women's dressing room."

"Okay. Fine with me. I will be there soon."

We hung up the phone. I wondered what type of taste test she was talking about. I hoped that she didn't run my pussy into overdrive. I was getting so tired of all this fucking, licking, sucking. I never thought I would say that.

After dragging myself out of bed, I took a shower and got dressed. I walked next door to holla at Peaches before I headed out to the club.

"Hi, baby," she spoke while giving me a hug. The kids ran over and gave me hugs too.

Looking at what looked like all their shit in boxes, I asked "Are you all ready?"

"Of course! Don't you see all my things are in boxes? The kids are so ready to go. I can't wait to see Mississippi," she spoke in a sexual manner.

"Well, we stay in the country part of Mississippi. We live in a city called Forest. It's pretty boring, but it is home. Where is Pete?" I asked.

"He hasn't been home in such a long time. He told me that he wants a divorce."

"Really?" I said out loud, because from within, it hit me he hadn't done what I told him to do.

"That weak bitch! He won't even answer my phone calls."

"He has changed his phone number so I won't call him."

"Well, fuck Pete. We will make it together. Just have everything ready. I'm going to get in contact with the moving people to pack all my things and grab your things. I guess you all can move in with me until we move, or vice versa. Or we all can get a hotel until we move," I stated.

"That's very nice of you, Christina, to move me and the kids with you." I guess I paused too long, because she was looking confused. "Why do you seem so agitated and pissed off?"

"I'm not pissed off, just a little tired."

"You must have had a long night." I said to Dave as I settled in to the car.

"Not really. My wife was acting like a bitch last night. She argued all night. You women don't let shit die down."

"Damn, Dave. I didn't know you were married."

"Yes, I am. For the last ten years, and that bitch is driving me crazy. I'm so tired of hearing her fucking mouth. I wonder what in the hell I can do to make her shut the fuck up?"

"Well, you can listen. Here me out. Just listen to what she is saying. Don't act like you listen and you're really not hearing her," I spoke.

"Listen. I do that, but she still runs off at the fucking mouth."

"You mean you act like you listen. Seriously, just listen and act like you want to hear what she is talking about."

"How do you know? I'm way older than you, shawty."

"I know, Dave, because I do it to my boyfriend all the time. When I acted like I was listening, he would stop all that bullshit-ass talking," I laughed.

We both began laughing and he asked, "Do your boyfriend know about you out here whoring around?"

"Whoring? Maybe we can use another word," I laughed.

"Shit. There is no other word. That's what it is."

"Hell no, he doesn't know. I need to hurry up and end this shit before I get busted. He already threatened to come up here and fuck me up," I laughed.

"Damn, girl. You better wrap this shit up," Dave spoke.

We both laughed out loud again and finally pulled up at the club. I walked in with my million dollar face and we proceeded to the office. Before we could reach the office door, I was looking at

men sucking and fucking each other everywhere. Big dicks, small dicks, damn! I wanted to get involved, but they didn't want me. I say more power to them. Fuck and suck each other until the sun comes up.

Mrs. Lee was standing by Mr. Lee, as he said while walking out the door, "It's about time you got here. I was about to let the girls go home."

"What girls? The bitches you have in the back?" I spoke sarcastically.

"Yes, those bitches. Get relaxed and put all your things here."

"For what? You going to make all them eat my pussy?" I joked.

"No, baby. You are going to taste all their pussies tonight. Since you enjoyed Cherry last night, I want you to taste them all and pick the one you love," she stated.

"Oh, hell yeah. I'm so ready to taste NeNe again. I bet that bitch has some bomb-ass pussy."

Mrs. Lee grabbed my arm when I mentioned tasting NeNe, and from the way she did it, you would think she and I were lovers. Staring into her eyes, I felt lost, and from my expression to her I must have looked confused, because I was.

"Get this straight, Christina - I don't want you tasting other pussy but mines, and if you think it's a game, try me."

"Whoa, wait one minute. You called me in here to taste pussy, and if you know me like you do, then you know that I intend to taste pussy."

She looked at me and replied as she got in my face, "I made you and I will break you. Your body belongs to me, and only me. Is that understood? As a matter of fact, all of you bitches get the fuck out…except for you!"

"Why are you so possessive, when there are other bitches that have been here longer than I have?" I said as I looked from her face to my arm.

"It's not often that I come across a bad pussy-eating freak like you, and I have you. I'd be a damn fool to let you trick out these bitches that work for me."

"Are you forgetting that you are married, with a business to run?"

"Since the day I tasted you, I knew you were mine. As for my husband, he's not stupid, and as far as my business, you are my business. Let's proceed to the dressing room, shall we? You will do as I said, and if you look like you are enjoying yourself, you will be punished. You hear me, bitch?" Mrs. Lee asked as she clapped her hands together and led the way down the dark, gloomy hall, not quite expecting an answer.

That was the longest walk of my life. *Here I am with a chance to taste the pussy of bitches that think they are the shit, and now*

my boss wants me to look but not touch. I don't think so, I thought as we continued walking.

We walked to the dressing room, and I saw a small circle platform with legs in mid-air. I was like a fucking nigga in heat, wanting to fuck or do something to somebody, but Mrs. Lee's words were alive in my ear. I proceeded to put on my two piece bikini suit, and yes, I added a bib as a final touch.

I walked up the four steps into the taste testing area. They were in a semi-circle, and they looked at me. Their top halves were on this plush purple marble covered top that allowed them to lay back. Their feet were held apart by hangers that slanted their bodies, so that their pussies could hang in mid-air and let me have my way. I walked on the platform, first looking down at them, then responding as the door was being closed, "Yeah, bitches, it's time for me to demonstrate why I am the bad bitch at the mutherfucking club, and when I am finished, you're going to want to fuck me too." I looked back at Cherry as she stood with her arms crossed to make sure she heard me too, and from the looks of it, she did.

Turning around and getting off the platform, I really had no clue how this was going to work, but when I walked down the steps and made it back to Mrs. Lee, she asked me in a tone that dared me to put my tongue in them, "Are you pleased with the grade of pussy I have waiting on you to taste?"

"Mrs. Lee, I am very pleased, I am overwhelmed, and can't wait to start either."

In a whispery tone in my ear, Mrs. Lee said, "You are the best I have had in years, and only the best for my best, Christina. Don't forget what I said to you, try me…you are already sounding too eager, and I can shut this shit down at any second."

I smiled to play off the harmful words she told me before we got to the dressing room, and for some reason I believed her. Ever since she and I had been doing a little tasting here and there, she acted like we were more than employer and employee. I looked at Mrs. Lee and asked politely in her ear, "May I please do Cherry? I want to teach Paris a lesson as to why I am the bad bitch at Delicious Divas."

She responded, "Since you asked and I am here to stop it, go on, but play fair."

While Paris was still staring at me, I decided to give her something to look at. I stopped in front of Cherry. She was Paris's right hand in everything that went on around here and she would get dealt with too.

"Cherry, are you ready for me to pop you?" I said seductively.

"How many licks do you think it will take?" she said to be smart, but I replied, "As many as you can stand."

Grabbing a chair, I commanded her to prop her left leg on it. Mrs. Lee said not a word; she only watched because she knows

that I don't play with pussy, I eat it up. Paris tried to leave, but Mrs. Lee told her to stay for the show. Paris couldn't help but watch, even if she did not want to. Cherry's pussy was bulging out and ready to be tasted. I got down on one knee and began sniffing her first. I sniffed and sniffed. There wasn't a smell to it at all. I expected to smell some type of smell-good but none was to be found. It looked a little raunchy, and to be on top in the business, pussy was pussy. Cherry was looking down at me as my gaze held hers. Using my thumb, I flicked at her clit, and she budged just a little. Inserting my thumb a few more times, I tasted her, and a bit of cum ran down my fingers and into my hand. Making sure I did not waste any of her nectar, I used my hands like a cup and slurped it up.

The look in Cherry's eyes told me she wanted to feel my mouth, and I didn't make her wait. My tongue was wet from her cream, and I used it to make her clit sticky. Whenever my tongue raked over the hard clit, juice spilled down her legs. I licked it up to her pussy, as always making sure none went to waste. Doing this new way of revenge on bitches that have done nothing but talk about me, made me tingle on the inside. My pussy began to jump and bang like no tomorrow.

Cherry would rock and sway to my tongue, because her body was adjusting to my way of pleasure. No longer could I ignore how my tongue felt. It was slimy wet, as I continued to take Cherry's

body for a joy ride. Touching and squeezing her breasts with her left hand, she put her right hand on my head and pulled me deeper into her goods. All I could think about was going deeper into her, making the pussy fart from the pressure I wanted to give, and for her to nut on my face because of the pleasure I gave. I loved that shit. Whenever she came, she smashed my head into her pussy, holding her spot with my tongue on her, just to make sure I didn't miss a drop of juice, like a good bitch didn't.

"That's enough for now, Christiana and Cherry," Mrs. Lee spoke angrily.

Getting off my knees, I spanked Cherry on the ass.

Mrs. Lee looked at me as she spoke harshly, "Did her pussy taste good, Christina?"

Staring at Cherry, I licked my lips and responded, "Yes, the pussy tasted good, but can I talk to you alone?"

Mrs. Lee ordered everyone to leave and replied, "You followed orders well, and I am very pleased, Christina."

Quickly, without thinking, she snatched me up and said, "I am the boss here and I run this bitch. Don't ever ask to taste pussy in here unless I tell you, and if I don't tell you, then don't ask. Do you hear me?"

"Yes, I hear you."

She slapped me down, and as I fell, I hit my head on the chair. Mrs. Lee did not help me up; she only replied as she walked off by stepping over me, "Now you hear me."

I felt violated and abused because as bad as I was, fear was all over me. All I could think about was running, and as I ran, Paris was in my way. She blocked me as I started crying and she said, "I don't know who made you cry, but I am glad."

"What you mean, Paris?" I said between the tears.

"I brought you here to help you out, not to help me out the fucking door."

"I still don't understand."

"Since you been here, you have been fucking my bitches, and now I am old news, but that shit is about to change."

"Who is it that I'm supposed to be fucking, who has left you alone?" I said as my mind sped in high gear.

"You are fucking my bitch, Mrs. Lee, and now I am fucking your bitch."

"What you mean, you are fucking my bitch?"

"Peaches just don't grow in Georgia, now they grow here too."

My tears were going away as she mentioned fucking Peaches, so I retaliated and replied, "It does not matter, because I'm fucking the one you really want. I can find another peach; can you find another Mrs. Lee?"

I walked off fast, but Dave stopped me outside and replied, "That girl Peaches was tricked by Paris's lies. Paris told her that you did not want her, and she believed it for some reason. So don't say anything to her, let her tell you, okay?"

"Why do you even care? How do you know all of these things?"

Seeing Dave's seemingly-offended face, gave light to everything. I now understood the expression "Watch the dog that carries that bone". For the whole time Paris was telling me information on them, she was telling information on me. That bitch would pay the ultimate price, no matter what the cost. I didn't even give a fuck anymore.

Chapter 17

"Dave, could you go on and pick up Christina and take her to her destination? I have an important matter to discuss with this individual."

"Yes, I will give her a call when I get in the car and tell her that I am coming early."

"Thank you."

When Dave left, the man handed Mrs. Lee some pictures and said, "This boyfriend of hers is trouble, and the company he keeps is worse than that. I would advise you to let her go back to the South."

"Well, I don't pay you to give me advice; I pay you to gather useful information. And why are you telling me about a man who is far away?"

"The word on the street is that he plans to come here to see what his beloved Christina has been up to, and from the looks of him, he does not travel alone or light."

"He is irrelevant to me at this point. What did you find out about Paris and her girlfriend Peaches?"

The investigator lit a cigarette and said, "This Paris is only messing around, or shall I say, she *was* messing around with Peaches, because she was jealous of Christina. However, this Peaches is the same friend that Christina sees when she needs a female companion."

"Thank you, your work has been worth the while, but let me know if this so-called boyfriend tries to come here."

"Sure will."

They shook hands and he left, but Mrs. Lee sat in her chair and began thinking of how to keep Christina away from those people.

I didn't want to think about what I didn't have. I received a call around six o' clock from Dave that he was coming early to take me to Mr. Justin Moore's home.

When Dave arrived early, I did not question him, because at this point, I felt that this was all Mrs. Lee's doing. He had to wait for a few minutes so I could be completely fresh. I told Dave to take me on to my next appointment. During the entire time, I kept thinking about how Mrs. Lee had been acting. I really did not like it, but she is the bitch that makes shit happen, and I needed her on

my team until I decided to give this up. As that thought crossed my mind, I realized that I hadn't heard from Pierre. I called him, but it went straight to his voicemail. *How odd*, I thought.

That thought quickly went away, as we were arriving at Justin's house, and from the outside, I knew it was totally different. He met me at the door and took off my jacket to reveal my off-the-shoulder dress. He kissed my shoulder and took me by the hand like a real man.

My arm was in his, as we walked down a very bright hallway. I looked down, and the floor was made of dark cherry wood; the scent of fresh flowers was everywhere. Famous pictures were all over the living area. We made our way to a dining room that had a huge chandelier above the medium square table, and accent paintings of angels shooting arrows were on the ceiling. *How creative! Who would have thought of such a thing?* I thought.

"You have a very interesting home," I replied as I looked around at the artifacts and drawings.

"Thank you. I have traveled all over the world and have acquired many things, but you being here makes this house a treasure I don't have yet," he replied ever so politely.

I could only blush, because no one has ever said anything like that to me. Feeling good about wanting to fuck him, I smiled a gracious smile. He pulled the chair out for me and spoke, "I have prepared a meal for us to eat first, if you don't mind."

"That's very sweet of you. I am a little hungry for natural food," I said teasingly.

"Great! I have prepared some peppered steaks with baked potatoes and rolls. For dessert, we will have strawberry yogurt with freshly picked strawberries, and a 1933 white wine bottled - shocked of course."

"1933 was a good year for wine, it sounds delicious to me. What's the occasion?"

As he walked over to the sink to wash his hands, I did the same and then he replied to my question, "It's not every day a man like myself entertains a beautiful woman such as yourself. Therefore, it's the best for the best; nothing is held back tonight for you."

With his eyes on me, I took my hands, started from my face to pull my hair back, and tied it upon my head to reveal my slender neck and wonderful breasts. *To tease him a little*, I thought.

"You are very beautiful, and if you belonged to me, I would never let you out my sight," he said in a nervous tone.

"Tonight, pretend that I am only yours, and don't let me out your sight," I said, as I looked at him seductively.

"Thank you, Ms. Christina, I will keep that in mind," he said.

"You're welcome," I said with glee in my eyes.

Justin pulled out my chair and then fixed our plates. He took out the steak knife and cut my steak into small pieces. He

reminded me so much of Pierre. *That's what he would do*, I thought.

Afterwards, he seated himself. Justin said grace and we proceeded to eat. We talked and talked, until he grabbed the plates and put them in the washer. We cleaned the kitchen together, and then he grabbed me, kissing me passionately. As we kissed, he began undressing me.

"What about dessert?" I said huskily.

"You are my dessert, Christina," he said in a deep voice.

He took his time undressing me, but soon I was standing in the middle of the floor naked. Justin picked me up and placed me on this huge dinner table. He walked over to the refrigerator and took out the yogurt. Smiling, Justin came back over and began spreading the strawberry yogurt over my naked body. He dipped his fingers in and spread it gently over my breasts, making my nipples stand like they were marching for war. Placing yogurt on my thick, bald pussy, he then used his tongue to spread more yogurt on my body. His thick tongue had my full attention, and I couldn't wait for him to lick more.

Justin put down the bowl and began licking me everywhere. Starting at my toes, he sucked each of them one by one. He made each toe feel that they were special. He took his time and took care of my feet. I didn't think I could walk, because I felt limp and weak. He noticed the yogurt was sliding down my sides and

running down my breasts, and he moved his attention to them. As his tongue ran over me, he bypassed my pleasure spot and sucked my breasts. He was kind to them at first, then very aggressive with them. He grabbed them both up with a firm grip and pulled my nipples. I moaned out then spoke, "Shit, that hurt."

"I'm so sorry, baby. Didn't mean to make it hurt."

"Please slow down. You have me for tonight, and we have all night. I am not going anywhere you don't want me to go," I told him, as he looked at me with sorrow.

"I know. It's just that I haven't been with a woman for a year, and I get impatient. Actually, I'm so excited," he said, in an honest tone.

"I do understand that, but please take it easy, I am here for you," I replied.

I spread my legs as far as I could, because he needed to see how beautiful a woman like me looked on his expensive table. He stood between my legs and tenderly touched my spot. He took his tongue and tasted me without the extra food, and it was gentle. Justin then took both hands and dipped them into the yogurt, buttering my pussy like a biscuit. He sat on the chair and before him like a dinner plate was my pussy. Justin took soft nibbles of my pie and increased his movement. The loving way his tongue caressed my pussy made something stir inside me. Flicking back and forward was the huge tongue all over my pussy, and he got

carried away and took it deep inside me. I moaned because he was really using his tongue on me, and I loved the way it went back and forth from my clit to my ass. Adding more yogurt to me, he crushed up the strawberries and began to eat the white desert off me. Justin did it very romantically and with caution.

He was gentle with me, and as my toes wiggled back and forth, I yelled out as I came quickly. Justin watch the cum run down my thighs with delight, and he licked from my thighs to my ass and then the warm spot that released the white creamy filling. My kitty purred like someone was rubbing my fur. Justin took his hand and inserted it inside me a few times, and tasted me again. He went to town on that pussy. He knows how to suck a clit and tongue fuck me. *If he isn't a pro, I don't know one*, I thought as he had my head spinning, while he was expertly sucking on my clit. Justin finished tasting me again, and I did not think I could take much more of a man taking his time loving my pussy.

Barely looking up, I saw him pulling off he pants. Hanging between his legs was a huge-ass dick, swaying back and forth like a branch in the wind. He stood up with his huge dick fully erect and ready to dig deep inside me. With no warning at all, Justin began beating that dick up against my clit. It felt heavy and hard against me, and second thoughts came to my mind. I had to get a good look, and this time when I looked at him, that mutherfucker was at least eleven or twelve inches. He had a fucking horse dick. I

see why he doesn't get pussy that often. *Who is going to let this big dick mutherfucker fuck them?* I thought. Then I thought about pretending to faint to get out of it, but I wanted to see how a monster dick like that would feel, plunging deep in me and taking control. I hope he knew how to work it.

"Come here," Justin spoke, as he dipped his dick in the yogurt bucket.

"Yes, Big Daddy. Anything for you, tonight is your night, do what you feel," I spoke.

I got off the table and watched his dick hang close to his knees, as I looked him over - mind you, he's not a short man. Picking up his dick with both hands, I looked at his mushroom cap and felt delighted at the thought of it. It was swollen and pinkish, with no hair covering it at all. I bent down to suck him, and Justin looked down at me, as I tried to stuff his entire massive dick into my mouth. It was hard, but I managed. After taking him in fully, I removed my mouth and began to lick all around like a lollipop on a stick.

Finally, Justin picked me up and carried me to the bedroom, and laid me across this big-ass queen-size bed that was soft and fluffy. I seemed to fall deep into the comforter set. We gazed into each other's eyes, as if we had fallen in love with each other. He reminded me so much of Pierre. The things he did and the things he said made me feel so good. He laid me on the bed with yogurt all over me. Placing me on the bed, Justin caressed, sucked, licked, and kissed every inch of my body. I mean, he kissed my body from head to toe. He was generous with his lovemaking, and I accepted him entirely.

In haste, Justin mounted me and began stuffing his dick in my small pussy. He pushed and tugged at me, and my pussy could not take all that meat he was packing. Justin was truly a massive man, and he knew that, but I stood like a solider.

The more he drove deeper into me, the more I began to cry out, and not in pain, but for more. Justin stuffed me, and twisted me over and over. *If only I could see how much of his gigantic dick I was really taking*, I thought. *If only I could be a fly on the wall...* But those thoughts were interrupted by him stuffing me like a turkey on Thanksgiving Day. Overall, it didn't hurt as bad as I thought, because he knew how to stroke a bitch like me. For hours on end, we stroked each other until he busted nut after nut on my stomach. Each nut he busted on me, I would play in it, and to entice him, I would taste his seed and he would smile.

"No one has ever taken all of me before," Justin said with amazement.

"You have never had anyone like me that is willing to take a man like you," I said, but in truth, I was sore, and he may have pulled my uterus down or halfway out by the way he was taking me.

"Let's take a shower together," he suggested.

"I would love that, thank you, Justin" I said as I still laid there, not moving.

"Great," he stated.

He noticed that I was still in bed; therefore, he began to carry me to the shower. As we entered this huge-ass bathroom, my eyes lit up. I looked up at this window ceiling, and it shone like pure gold. "Absolutely beautiful," I thought. He continued to carry me over to the shower and placed me in it. Justin fixed the shower at a reasonable temperature and we showered. He washed my body, as I washed his. This was like a romance story. All this shit felt good, but it reminded me so much of Pierre. I had to get home to my King. I had to leave this lifestyle and go home to the man that I have always loved.

After we showered, Justin took me to bed and held me. He didn't try to fuck me again. In fact, I don't think I could take any more of his huge-ass dick. My pussy needed a break, especially after that dick I took from him. He kissed the back of my neck and caressed my breasts until I fell asleep. It felt so good to finally be appreciated by a man that recognized when he was in the presence of a real woman. Around four o'clock in the morning, I felt Justin hands squeezing my breasts. He began kissing my neck roughly. His dick was very hard and aching, ready to take me. He entered me from the back and rushed me with no warning at all. For a few

minutes as he took me, I pulled away and turned him towards me, trying to make him get on top. He flipped over on top and began fucking me fiercely. He reached under my shoulders and grabbed me tightly, ramming his big dick inside me without concern for whether he was tearing me or not. Justin pushed and pushed more and more of that huge dick inside me, until I cried out for him to stop.

My cries felt good to him, and this caused Justin to stroke harder and stroke deeper in my pussy walls, taking my canal to another level of rough loving. Whenever I thought he was finished, he would reach all the way back by placing his dick at the edge of my pussy, then take it out and rush that dick on me full force. Hardcore fucking me went on for hours between Justin and I; he seemed not to take a break, and he kept going. It was as if he took some type of Viagra or whatever it was; ordinary was not the case. My legs felt heavy and trembled from Justin's way of loving, and the sweat poured off us like water. I thought I would suffocate with the heat our bodies brought on. The more he humped, the wetter the bed got.

After hours of love making, he came all over me, and I was too exhausted to enjoy the spilling of his seed. He got out of the bed and he took all the covers off, as if nothing had happened. *His stamina is off the chain*, I thought as I watched him move with a lot of energy.

After that, we took another shower and he put me in the guest bedroom. I could hear him cleaning up his house, going from room to room. After listening for awhile, I fell asleep.

When I woke up, I looked at the clock and it read one o' clock. "Oh fuck, what the hell! I have overslept," I said to myself.

I jumped out of the bed and got dressed. I looked around the house for my purse. It lay on the Queen Anne coffee table. Reaching inside to look at my phone, I noticed that there were several calls from Pierre. I didn't call back, but shoved the cell back in my purse. Walking over to the balcony windows, I could see Justin outside washing off his Suzuki motor bike. He looked so handsome with those black jeans and no shirt. His muscles were in all the right places. My pussy began to ache again just looking out at him. He looked up and saw me. I waved to him and he waved for me to come out.

As I stepped out next to him, he spoke, "You admiring my bike?"

"No baby, your bike is not what I was daydreaming about," I joked as I touched his crotch.

"Okay. I see you didn't get enough of me last night. You are a woman who's hard to pleasure, I see," he replied.

"No, I'm not. I just like what I see, and you just happen to be in my sight right now - every inch of you."

Justin took the water hose and began spraying me with the water. He chased me around the bike, putting water all over me. The few clothes that I had on were soaking wet. Justin pulled me up to him and began kissing me. I received his tongue like I did last night. He let the water hose glide water down my soft breasts. He looked down at me and glided the water over each breast. Tossing the hose down, he took off my shirt and bra, caressing each breast with his warm mouth.

This soft loving is the Justin I remembered, I thought as he took ease with me.

"Get up on the bike," he requested.

"It will fall with me up there," I said, because I had never sat on a bike without anything attached to it.

"No, it won't fall. It's on the kickstand, and plus I have it where it won't move," he said teasingly. "Just get your fine ass up there. I want to taste you," he replied.

While taking my panties off in a teasing fashion, I replied, "Yes, Big Daddy," then I climbed on the bike backwards, lifting my skirt to expose my pussy.

I put both of my legs in the downward position and watched Justin's big tongue hang out of his mouth. Just thinking about how big all of him really is gave me the shivers; I felt the chills escalade up and down my body.

Justin caressed my bald pussy with his hand first, then he allowed his heavy tongue to hang out of his mouth to tease me. I didn't have long to imagine; he began banging his tongue down on my clit. My toes widened as his tongue grinded on that clit, to warm me up for the next stage of biting my pussy all over. They weren't ordinary bites, but bites of bliss. Before I could spring a nut on that face of his he stopped, picked up the hose, wetting me up. I could only laugh.

He pulled off his pants and told me to lie on the concrete. I looked at that mutherfucker as if he had lost his damn mind, but I remembered who was paying for a damn good time and how expensive it was. I didn't want to, but I did as he asked and laid my bare ass on the hard ass concrete. He stuck his big dick inside my pussy, and stroked me over and over again. Even though he was rough last night, my pussy seriously missed his dick. It didn't take long for me to get dripping wet with fluids, and he stroked me easy, making me cum faster than before.

When I got the first nut, Justin gathered my legs and placed them on his shoulders, exposing nothing but pussy to his swollen dick. I knew he was about to take advantage of the chance to make bruises on my back, but he didn't. Justin held his head backwards and made passionate love to me. This felt so right. He made up to this pussy for the brutal way he treated her, and I fully accepted his apology. My pussy stayed wet and moist for him, and when we

cried out together, we stared into each other's eyes as the big explosion rolled off my stomach and breasts.

He squirted like we had never fucked before, and to repay him, he got up and leaned against the bike as I took his wide, soft dick in my mouth and caressed his nuts with my hand. He moaned as I sucked like a baby with a bottle. He pushed me back, making giggling noises.

"What's wrong?" I asked him, because he had pushed me off him.

"It's so sensitive after you cum, and the way you pulling on me, a man would kill for it."

Stunned at his words, I smiled and replied. "Oh really?"

As I tried to reach for that dick again to put in my mouth, Justin jumped back and began to walk around, shaking his legs one at a time like a dog. I jumped on Justin's back, and he carried me inside the house.

He spoke, "Look up there."

"What?"

I looked up, and his neighbor had binoculars spying on us. We both started laughing. We both waved, and the old man jumped back behind the curtain.

"I really enjoyed your company, Christina," he stated.

"The same here. You are a wonderful man, and I hope you find the right woman for you one day."

"Yes. One day. I hope you find the right man too."

"I think I already have Justin. I have to go home and make this right between us. You will be the last person I sleep with," I surprisingly spoke.

"That's great. Congratulations," he spoke.

He dried my clothes, fixed me dinner, and I went home. Out of all this bullshit I have been through with, Justin will be the one I will never forget.

Chapter 18

Dave pulled up in a white Range Rover sitting on 24's. *Who in the fuck gave him a nice ride to pick me up?* I thought as I jumped in the vehicle, and he pulled off fast with the wheels wailing again. "Girl, I thought you were never going to leave that nigga's house. You have so much drama going on at the club."

"What kind of drama are you talking about?" I asked.

"I would tell you, but I love me. My job is to bring you to the club, and I am sorry, Christina, but I must bring you."

"Dave, you're making me nervous."

"You have a right to be; believe me, you have a right to be."

"Can we make a stop by Peaches' before you take me to the hotel?"

Thinking it over, he then said, "Fine, for a few minutes, but hurry up."

We made it to Peaches' place, and it was vacant. Nothing was seen, not even the blinds on the windows. I began to have an awful feeling in the bottom of my stomach, and from Dave's actions, something was really going on. Getting back into the truck, we traveled fast, so I called Pierre and there was no answer. I called Paris and still no answer from her either. *I know that bitch isn't fucking my main man*, I thought as we whizzed into the parking lot of the hotel.

Dave jumped out and ran off. Before I said anything, Pierre's goons ran up to the vehicle and escorted me up. This was some major shit. He had never rolled up on me like this. I guess I had never pissed him off before like this either. This guy with a scar across his face opened the door and pushed me in. I looked back at him as he closed the door. His white friend Michael got off the couch and blocked the front door. I was looking around for Pierre, and there he came from the back with this ugly-ass face I have never seen before.

"What's all this bullshit you have going on around here," I spoke.

"Bitch, you have lost your mutherfucking mind!" he yelled, while snatching me up by my collar. "What the fuck is this bitch Paris talking about?"

"Pierre, I don't know what you are talking about! How can you ask me what she is talking about, and I don't even know what she

said. And of all people, you're gonna listen to Paris?" I said nervously, and also afraid, because I have never seen Pierre so pissed off before, until now.

"Don't fucking play with me right now, Christina. You know damn well what the fuck I'm talking about."

"Why would I fucking lie to you, Pierre. I'm a grown-ass woman?"

"I don't know bitch, you tell me."

As fast as a lion on weaker prey, Pierre jumped on me and clamped his fingers tightly around my slender neck to choke me. I tried to put my hands through his, to pull his fingers away from around my neck. His grip was tight, but I managed to speak, "Get the fuck off me, nigga."

"You mean to tell me this fucking job you need requires you to eat bitches' pussy and suck niggas' dick?" he continued to yelled.

"I'm not doing shit, nigga!"

"Really!" he screamed as he shoved me down on the floor. "Look at these mutherfucking pictures that were sent to me!" he screamed, slapping me in the face with pictures. I grabbed the pictures and began looking through them. Every one of them pictures showed me eating pussy. There were none of me sucking dick, but of one with the guy fucking me on stage. My heart fell down to my panties. This nigga is going to kill me. I rubbed my throat and Pierre kicked the pictures out of my hand.

"Get the fuck up before I beat your ass."

"I'm not doing shit. Get the fuck out! You and your fucking goons get the fuck out my shit! Can't you see the pictures are altered?" I stood up, yelling.

Pierre slapped me so hard across the face, sending me back to the floor. As he sat on my chest area, facing me, he then had a clear open view of my face, which he slapped repeatedly while saying, "Bitch, I love your fake ass. What the fuck are you doing, man?"

"Get off me, Pierre" were the only words I could mumble, because my vision was becoming blurry and my mind was disorientated.

"Shut the fuck up," he screamed, as he continued to slap me in the face. With an opportunity available, I bucked him off me and covered my head as I curled up. He snatched me up off the floor and grabbed my hair. He pulled my hair so hard, I thought my scalp was coming loose. He pulled me in the bedroom and slammed the door. Pierre shoved me on the bed and I turned around, trying to fight him back. He forced me down on the bed and grabbed me around the neck. "I fucking love you, Christina. How could you do this fucking shit to me?" he spoke, as tears came down his face. He was choking me so much harder than before, as tears fell down my face.

As I begun to lose consciousness, all kinds of thoughts ran across my mutherfucking mind. If Pierre didn't kill me, Paris would get beat down this time around. I wasn't going to let that bitch make it. Something told me not to trust that mutherfucking bitch. I wanted to pick up the phone and dial her number, but I knew she wouldn't answer. When I did get free enough to call, I was going to leave her a nasty-ass voicemail. But first I had to live through Pierre's ass whipping.

Chapter 19

When I woke up, the room was very dark. I began coughing and trying to throw up. The light came on, and Pierre was sitting there staring at me.

"Are you all right?" he asked as if remorseful about it.

"No. I need some water," I continued, as I coughed while trying to hold it in.

"Baby, I'm so sorry for losing my head earlier. I can't believe that you came all the way up here in Denver to be a whore. You could have done that at home," he spoke.

"Whore? Why don't you just leave me alone? As you see I'm no good, and I'm not wifey material. Go out and find them other bitches you have been fucking."

"You're right; I have been fucking other bitches. At least they are honest and fucking me, and going home. You were supposed to be my main bitch. My down bitch, but instead, you fucking other freaky fuckers, and bitches too from the pictures," he replied.

"Since you have been fucking other bitches, get the fuck out of here!" I screamed, as I jumped up and tried to run out the door. Pierre grabbed me from the back and began trying to hold me down. "Get the fuck off me, Pierre! I don't want you anymore. Get the fuck out!" I continued to yell.

"Baby, you know you still love me. I should beat your fucking ass, but I'm not going to, because I have been wrong too. I feel that it is partially my fault that you had to stoop to this degree of getting money. I could have helped you start your own business or something, and watch you make that dough, but I didn't think like that."

"Pierre," I spoke as I broke down crying. Falling down to the floor, Pierre went down with me, and we cried. He cried harder than I did.

"I'm so sorry, Christina. I promised my parents I would love you forever. I can't let you go."

"I'm sorry too, Pierre. Baby, please forgive me. I want to go home and become your wife, if you still want me?" I asked.

"Yes, baby. That's what I want. I want us to be together as one. We will get past this…this is true. But next time, I will kill your ass," he stated.

"Yes baby, we can get past this," I responded after looking at him and choosing my words wisely.

Pierre and I sat there, and I cried until there were no more tears. He rubbed my hair and stared into my eyes. It's like we were in love all over again. This is the man I wanted to be my husband. There was nothing in the world that could take his place. Not even Peaches. My heart belonged to Pierre. After my cries, we walked out to the living room. It was around eleven o'clock at night. He told everyone to go back to the hotel, until we left tomorrow. Everyone moved kind of slowly. Finally, they disappeared. We were left alone.

Sitting down at the kitchen table, he spoke, "So who is this Peaches?"

Looking at him, I spoke, "She's the next-door neighbor."

"Are you fucking her too? Don't you dare lie either!"

"I wasn't going to lie, baby. She's a female I have been with."

"What you mean 'been with'?"

"Someone I have fucked," I spoke, as I swallowed hard. I could see his jaw clench, but he asked for the truth, and no way was I going to lie now and get another beat down.

"And you trying to take her back to Mississippi with us?" he asked.

"How did you know that?" I asked.

"Because she came over here looking for you. She had her own key, and we talked for a few minutes," he spoke.

"Okay. What did she say? And where is that bitch now, anyway?"

"Nothing really, that you were moving her and the kids back with us."

"Is it okay if she comes back with us? Her and her kids can live in my house, and I can move in with you," I spoke, knowing that's what he wanted to hear.

"Yeah, that's cool with me, or you can move her in with us and we can both fuck her," he spoke, trying to see my reaction.

"That would be good too. You can have me and her to fuck, instead of them bitches out in the streets."

"Yeah, that would be great. In-house pussy like a mutherfucker," he laughed.

I looked into his face, and he was very excited about the idea. I wanted to ask him about the bitches he was fucking, but didn't want to be disappointed. It would hurt me like hell to find out if one of them bitches was a friend of mine, so I let it slide.

I looked at him as I walked out and proceeded to the bed. I lay across the bed and stared out the window. It was a full moon. The

man I wanted to be my husband would be fucking me and another woman. At first, it seemed like a good idea. But now as it swirled around my head, it didn't seem like a good idea. I love Peaches and I love Pierre. I didn't know if I wanted to share him though. It would only be fair, because I would still be fucking her too.

Hearing the door crack open, I closed my eyes as if I was sleeping. Pierre got on the bed next to me and curled under me like a little baby. As I lay very still, I could hear him cry. He held me tighter and cried himself to sleep. Damn, all this was my fault.

Chapter 20

The next morning, we took a shower together and headed out towards the club. Pierre hadn't said a word to me all morning. He called his goons to meet us at the club. I called Mrs. Lee ahead of time to warn her that we were coming. Mr. Lee opened the club door, and we walked in like we were robbing the place. Pierre had me by the hand. Dave stood tall, pointing to the office. We walked through the door, and two bodyguards stood next to Mrs. Lee as she sat down at her desk.

"How may I help you, sir?" she asked Pierre.

"I'm taking Christina away from here. How much do I have to pay?"

"I don't want you to pay me a mutherfucking thing. I want Christina. She has the best-tasting pussy in this club, and has even topped all my money makers in sales."

Pierre looked at me and I put my head down. I didn't want to see that hurting expression on his face, but this was what he wanted. "I don't give a fuck what you want. You can't have her. How much will it take for you to disappear out of our lives?"

"You must have misunderstood me. Christina signed a contract. If she breaks the contract, you will have to pay $100,000. Can you afford that?" Mrs. Lee spoke sarcastically.

Pierre snapped his fingers, and one of his goons brought forward a Nike duffle bag. He reached in the bag and counted, "20, 40, 60, 80, and 100. That's 200 stacks; now we about to be out. Do we have an understanding?"

"Let's be clear. I run this shit around here, and I do what I please…and Christina pleases me," Mrs. Lee said, clearly testing him.

Pierre pulled his Glock .45 and then the rest of the niggas pulled out their guns. Mrs. Lee, Damien, and the bodyguards pulled out guns. These niggas were about to kill somebody. Damn, here goes the showdown.

"Pierre, don't," I spoke out. He pointed straight at Mrs. Lee's head, and she had her gun pointed at his head.

"Do we have an understanding here about fucking with my girl?"

Before Mrs. Lee could answer, I interrupted, "Yes she does, Pierre. I don't want to be a part of this life anymore."

"Are you sure?" Mrs. Lee asked me, raising her right eyebrow, almost sure that I would back down.

"Yes, I am very sure. I'm going on to marry Pierre. This lifestyle is not for me."

"Okay, then it's settled," Mrs. Lee replied, as she lowered her gun and told her crew to lower theirs.

Pierre and his goons put their guns away. "Now, Mrs. Lee, do we have an understanding?" he asked her, looking directly into her eyes.

"Yes, sir. I don't want to let her go, but I have no choice. You have bought her out of her contract."

"Where is this so called fucking contract?"

Mrs. Lee reached inside of her front desk and handed the papers to Pierre. He glimpsed over the papers and began to tear them to pieces. Mrs. Lee was about to walk out, when she stopped and stared into my face. I looked into her eyes and laid my head down on Pierre's chest like a small baby. She put her head down and started to walk out but stopped at the door, staring at us. Pierre and I turned our attention away from her and began staring at each other.

"Baby, I love you, and it broke my heart to know what you were up here doing with all those women and men. But I love you, and will never lose you to some bullshit like that. Let's go, we have our entire lives ahead of us."

221

I had never felt so happy, but before I could respond, the door opened and Peaches and Paris walked in with hats upon their heads. They were dressed in long trench coats, high heels, and looked seductive. They swung open their coats and lifted what appeared to be Glock .45 hand guns. In an instant, the lights went out, the office door flew open, and shots were being fired everywhere. Pierre's goons took out weapons as soon as the girls showed up as a threat. People were screaming and I was rushed to the floor, crawling around like a madwoman trying to find Pierre. He did not answer, so I knew all too well that he and his goons were shooting at Peaches and Paris. Suddenly, I became parallel to the floor and my stomach had a burning sensation. I could no longer hear what was going on. I felt very weak, tired, and short of breath.

The lights came back on and Pierre rushed over towards me quickly. He picked me up and began holding me, saying with tears, "Hang in there, baby, hang in there." He continued, "Somebody call for some fucking help."

I looked around the room, and bodies were lying out everywhere: Dave, Paris, two of Pierre's goons, and my Peaches. My eyes filled with tears as Pierre grabbed my face and turned my head back towards him.

His voice sounded faint and far away, as I stretched my ears, trying to listen. *What is he talking about, hanging in there?* I pondered.

He made an attempt to lift my hands to wipe away his tears, which was funny since I could not lift my hands and speak to him. I rolled my eyes to the right and saw police rushing in, then the paramedics behind them. I could feel Pierre straining to talk, as two of them walked over to us. They said something to Pierre. He did not respond, but moved as if he was holding something hot.

The paramedics were pulling on me, although, I could not feel or hear them. They started pumping on my chest and touching my wrist. *I know those bitches didn't shoot me?* I thought. With Pierre on my left side, they lifted me onto the stretcher. As they carried me out, I looked up and saw Mrs. Lee standing back by her office window. *How did that bitch manage not to get shot?* I thought. We stared at each other for a second, and she gave me this evil grin. Something wasn't right about all this shit. My thoughts rushed back to what Mrs. Lee had spoken once, "I made you, and I'll break you." This bitch set me up. As the paramedics took me to the ambulance and Pierre stood at my side, Mrs. Lee walked behind slowly, just staring.

They lifted me in the ambulance and closed the door. Pierre and I looked at Mrs. Lee through the glass, staring. She rushed up on the ambulance and opened the door before we began to take off.

We all looked at her with surprise when she lifted a black Glock .45 and opened fire. The ambulance driver went down. Pierre went down, and then she began to load my body with bullets. Blood oozed out my mouth, as I lay there helplessly.

Mrs. Lee spoke. "I told you, don't fuck with me. I made you, and I will break you." She put the gun in her mouth and pulled the trigger. Her body fell dead. I looked over at Pierre as he laid there dead. I gasped for breath, closed my eyes, and let go…

PUBLICATIONS PRESENTS

NICOLE'S FACE WAS SWEET AND INNOCENT,
BUT NIKKI'S REVENGE WAS UNSTOPPABLE...

A NOVEL BY
AMANDA LEE

A NOVEL BY
AMANDA LEE

n Deranged, Nikki achieved her goal of capturing
eremy for Nicole, but fell short as Cowboy spoiled their
lans. One year later, Nikki refuses to fail and no longer
eeds Nicole or her assistance. In Deranged 2, Nicole's
ace was sweet but Nikki s revenge was unstoppable as
he moved heaven & earth to be with her man and live
he dream life that they planned together. Once free,
ND she sees he's cheating and living their dream life
ith someone else, Jeremy and his family have nowhere
o hide. The question is: Will she finally get what she
ants or will she die trying?

Author Amanda Lee

www.authoramandalee.com

www.facebook.com/authoramandalee

www.twitter.com/diamez22

PUBLICATIONS PRESENTS

WELCOME TO THE JUNGLE

WHERE LOVE AND LOYALTY DON'T EXIST

NOW AVAILABLE

ENTER AT YOUR OWN RISK

WELCOME TO A WORLD WHERE A SIMPLE
CLICK CAN GET YOU SEX, MONEY, AND
EVEN MURDERED...

SPRING 2012

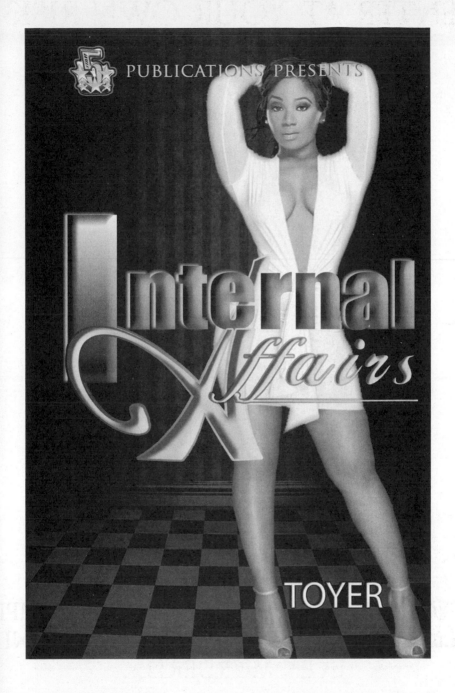

COMING SUMMER 2012

COMING FALL 2012